She's hiding something

Dear Diary:

Tonight at dinner I said to our new tenant, "I'll help you carry your things upstairs, Claudine." I thought this idea was pretty brilliant. Carrying her stuff up, I'd get to see what records and books she had. A true detective like me can gather a lot of information about a person from these sorts of clues.

"Oh, thank you," she said, "but I really have so little. It is easier to do it myself."

Diary, you are probably going to think I'm crazy, but instead of thinking she was just trying not to be any trouble to us, my first thought was: She's hiding something. There's something about Claudine that she doesn't want anybody to know!

Dear Diary

THE MYSTERY

Carrie Randall

AN
APPLE
PAPERBACK

SCHOLASTIC INC.
New York Toronto London Auckland Sydney

ISBN 0-590-44022-5

12 11 10 9 8 7 6 5 4 3 2 1   1 2 3 4 5 6/9

Printed in the U.S.A.   40

First Scholastic printing, January 1991

THE MYSTERY

KEEP OUT!!
(This means you!)

This diary is the property
of

Elizabeth Jane Miletti

ALL TRESPASSERS WILL BE
PROSECUTED!

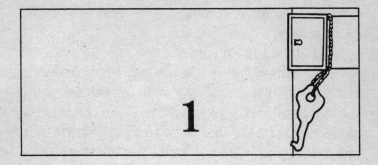

Dear **D**iary:

We had a painting party this afternoon at my house — me, my mom, my kid sister Darcy, and my best friend Nancy. This party was Mom's idea, and I'll admit I was suspicious at first. I thought it was just her crafty trick to get us all to help her fix up my grandmother's old attic apartment.

Now that Gram's married to Ralph Bagnold, and they are living in their own house, her old apartment is empty and my mother has been bursting with money-making ideas for using the space. But first we had to clean it up and patch the cracks in the plaster and wax the floors and paint the walls to get the place spruced up.

Mom came into my room on Friday night and said, "How about a painting party?!" and her voice was just filled with fun, as though she were asking, "Do you want to go to Disney World?" I knew, though, that she was just trying to put a sugar coating on the bitter pill of some big, awful chore.

"Just who all is coming to this *party*?" I said, being cagey.

"Darcy said she'd come."

Darcy is my sister. She's eight. She's fine as a sister — a little spacey, and sometimes *very* pesky, but mostly okay. Still, I can't say she's someone I'd be thrilled to go to a party with. For one thing, she talks too loud. For another, she's the world's worst dancer. Basically she thinks dancing means hopping around first on one foot, then on the other. I'd die of embarrassment if I had to actually go to a *real* party with her. But then I knew this wasn't a *real* party.

"Are Josh and Adam coming?" I said. One of my biggest complaints around our house is that my older brothers get off the hook from doing a lot of the chores, just because they're teenagers and have so many big, important things to do after school and on weekends. Things like sports, class projects, field trips. But this time, they had something worse to do than I did.

"Your brothers are going to help your dad clean out the basement," my mom said.

I didn't complain anymore. I'd rather paint Gram's apartment a hundred times than clean our basement, which is straight out of *Friday the 13th*, or *Nightmare on Elm Street*. It's really more of a dungeon than a basement. There are cobwebs in every corner, and you know what lives in cob-

2

webs. Plus there're tons of old junk down there — our junk but also junk from families who lived in our house way before us. There are probably a couple of dead bodies underneath everything. Murder victims from a hundred years ago. Unsolved crimes like the ones on TV. (I have a very vivid imagination — sometimes *too* vivid.)

"I'd *love* to come to the painting party. So nice of you to invite me," I said in my phoniest cheery voice, so my mom would know that I was just going along with this because I had to, not because I was falling for her trick.

Oh, well, I thought. Maybe it wouldn't be so bad. I knew that at least I could get Nancy to come. She really *would* think it was fun. She's an only child and her parents are separated, and so she thinks anything "family-ish" that we Milettis do is incredibly fun and heartwarming, and she loves to be asked to join in. I, on the other hand, think *her* house is heaven. Since there's only Nancy and her mother, they have these nice quiet dinners where they play classical music on the stereo while they eat. I love going over there. It's so calm and elegant. At my house, dinner is about as calm and elegant as a bowling alley.

Actually, Nancy and I envy practically everything about each other. I wish I were tall like she is, and had her long, straight blonde hair. (*Straight* is the part I envy most.) She wishes she

3

were short like me so she wouldn't be the butt of so many tall jokes. She'd love to have curly hair. And she'd especially like to have any name but her own. It's not the Nancy part. She doesn't mind that. It's her last name — Underpeace — that she'd love to ditch. For years, she's been teased with every possible variation. Underwater. Undertaker. Underwear. I've told her she can consider herself an honorary Miletti if that helps.

She's practically one of us anyhow. I mean, who else would've come to the painting party?!

As it turned out, the party actually *was* fun. Mostly on account of how bumbling we all were — kind of like the Three Stooges, only there were four of us. My mom forgot to tie a scarf around her head and wound up with pink speckled hair from standing under the roller when she painted the ceiling. I stepped right in the roller pan once and had to spend about half an hour scrubbing off my shoe. Darcy was the worst. I looked over once and she had *way* more paint on the floor in front of her — where she'd forgotten to put down newspapers — than she did on the wall she was wheeling her roller over. Actually, she was more *smooshing* the roller around than rolling it.

We were all goofing up. Even Nancy — who's incredibly neat — wound up doing all the trim on three windows before my mom noticed she'd done it all in the same pink paint we were putting on the walls.

"Uh-oh," my mom said. "I wanted that painted white."

Nancy groaned, but was a good sport and did it all over again.

In spite of stuff like this, we had fun listening to the radio, and talking, and taking turns sitting on the floor eating the sweet rolls my mother had made that morning for us. When we got sick of painting, we danced around to the music on the oldies station my mom likes. I've been pretty confident of myself as a dancer after I did so well at our school dance. Since then I've danced some more in front of the mirror up in my room, so I'm sort of in practice.

While we painted, we gossiped — first about Gram and Mr. Bagnold, her new husband. Gram would like me to call him "Grandpa Ralph," but I just can't bring myself to do that. I mean he's not my grandfather for one thing. For another, I barely know him. And to be perfectly honest (which I *always* am with you, Diary), I still resent him just a little, swooping in and getting my gram to run off and marry him, leaving us all behind. So for all these reasons, I call him Mr. Bagnold, although I think of him as Ralph. And he's really very nice.

"I call them Bill and Coo," I told everyone. "Because they're such lovebirds." Sometimes I can be kind of catty.

My mom shook her head. She still has trouble sometimes believing that her own mother just went and fell in love and got married and left home. Sometimes I think Mom thinks Gram's *her* daughter, instead of the other way around.

"In lots of ways your grandmother is acting like a young bride," Mom said. "As her daughter, it's a little hard getting used to. On the other hand, it's nice seeing her so happy again. And Ralph — do you notice he's putting on a bit of weight?"

"It's Gram's good cooking," I said. Ralph already had a little potbelly when he met Gram. Now he has a bigger one.

"She told me the way to a man's heart is through his stomach," Nancy said. Nancy and Gram are almost as good friends as me and Gram. Sometimes she knows things about Gram even I don't know, which is a little irritating. It seems I am having to share Gram with more and more people after years of having her pretty much to myself as my favorite person in the world. I've always thought I was Gram's favorite, too. I mean I *know* I'm her favorite grandchild, but I used to think I might be her favorite person, period. I guess Ralph occupies that spot now.

* * *

6

When we were done, we stood back and admired our work. The apartment looked great. All pink and white and cheery. Like a little cottage in the English countryside, although it was actually the attic of a big old house in the suburbs of Detroit.

"Who are we going to rent it to?" I asked my mom.

"I'm not sure yet. I thought maybe I'd advertise. Get a student from the junior college maybe. It would have to be one person who didn't have a lot of furniture or stuff. This place is cute, but it *is* small."

"I'm not sure I like the idea of having a total stranger living upstairs from us," I said. "What if he or she turns out to be a total ghoul? Or a werewolf?"

"Check out all prospective tenants for any suspicious hair on their hands," Nancy said.

"Or fangs," Darcy added. She saw a vampire movie one night when no one else was watching, and has checked her closet every night since before she'll get in bed.

We were all just kidding around, but it did make me stop and think about how it would be odd having a total stranger upstairs instead of Gram, who's really part of our family. It got me to wondering just *who* this person would turn out to be.

* * *

When we got cleaned up and went downstairs, my dad and Josh and Adam were done cleaning out the basement and Dad was cooking dinner for us all. Well, I say "cooking," but I actually mean "defrosting," which is about the only kind of cooking my dad does. He's a sales rep for Roth Frozen Foods, and is always using us as guinea pigs for new products the company is thinking of putting on the market. Sometimes this means a chance to be the first kids in the world to try neat stuff like cheese-flavored onion rings. Other times it means being the only poor suckers in the universe to eat oyster kebabs, or some other terrible idea that crept out of the Roth test labs that week. And so we all eyed the microwave with suspicion as it ticked down the minutes on whatever was lurking inside. Finally it pinged.

"*Voilà!*" my father said like a big-time chef as he whipped open the door of the microwave and pulled out a plate of the strangest-looking food item yet — brightly colored, extremely gooey triangles.

We all — me and my brothers and sister and my mom and Nancy — stood in silence, trying to figure out what this stuff was.

"Dessert pizza!" my dad shouted. "These here are strawberry, these are blueberry, and these are chocolate."

"I forgot I've got football practice," Josh said, heading for the door.

"I've got baseball practice," Adam said.

"Ha! Wrong season! Caught you!" my dad said and pinched Adam's collar and sat him down. "I'm really disappointed in you kids. Here I'm providing you with a historic moment, the first dessert pizza in America, and you're turning up your noses."

"I want some," said Baby Rose, who's four and will eat anything. Josh calls her the Human Garbage Disposal.

"One piece coming right up," my dad said. Eventually he talked the rest of us into trying dessert pizza, which was better than it sounded or looked, but still a little too weird to really *like*. It did put us in the mood for real pizza though, and eventually Mom called and ordered us two large ones, and we all sat around the table having just the kind of warm family dinner Nancy loves coming over for.

"Oh," my dad said to my mom when we were almost done, "I think I may have found you a tenant for the attic apartment. We have a new marketing consultant who's just been brought in from New York. Claudine Ferrand. She's just out of college, and new in town. She's been staying at the motel by the freeway for the past few weeks. I saw her notice up on the company bulletin board saying she needed an apartment." He pulled a little slip of paper out of his wallet and gave it to my mom. "Here's her number."

"What's she like?" my mom asked.

"Oh, she seems very nice. Smart, too. The dessert pizza was *not* her idea. I really don't know that much about her. Come to think of it, though, she *does* have these odd little fangs that come out at night."

"Oh, Daddy," Darcy said and started blushing while the rest of us laughed.

"Is she French?" Nancy asked. "Her name *sounds* French."

"She comes from Paris originally," my dad said. "But she went to college in New York, so I guess she's been in the States awhile."

France, I thought. A French person living right under our roof. It was kind of exciting. I could just imagine dropping it into conversation so Samantha and her gang would overhear. "Oh, yes, we have a *French* tenant. She wanted to live someplace chic and sophisticated in Hampton Point, and so she picked our house."

Oh, Diary. Who else could I tell these stupid fantasies to? I'd die if anyone else knew them. There are some things I can tell Mom, lots I can tell Gram, and a few more I can tell Nancy. But

10

the most private stuff is strictly between you and me.

P.S. Mom called Claudine right after dinner, and now she's supposed to come over Monday night to look at the apartment. I wonder what she'll be like? I like her name already. Claudine. I'd trade her's for mine any day. Lizzie. Yuck.

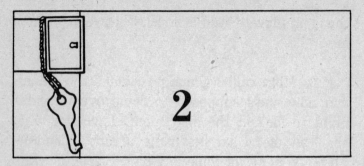

2

Dear **D**iary:

I hate Samantha Howard.

Because she has long, blonde perfectly curly hair. Because she thinks she's so cool and gorgeous. Because she *is* so cool and gorgeous. Because she's such a snob, always acting like the rest of us — regular kids like me and Nancy — are beneath her notice. Except when she wants something from one of us.

Like a while back, when she got this huge crush on my brother Adam and started acting like she was a big friend of mine, just so she could see more of him. She even talked me into having a pajama party so she could get a chance to hang out and flirt with him. Argh. I can still get mad just thinking about it. I just hate her.

So basically, I hate Samantha all the time, but today I hated her especially. She and her stupid friends Candace and Jessica all came to school dressed kind of matching. That is, they were all wearing striped sweaters and colored jeans, but each of their outfits was a different color. I think it was supposed to look like they were all in some secret club or something. They think they are *so* cool.

And then in the lunchroom, they played a practical joke on Tanya Malone. While she was in line getting milk, they switched her lunch bag for one with a trick sandwich in it — onions and Limburger cheese. When she sat down and opened it up, the smell was so gross it drove off all the other kids at her table. Meanwhile Samantha and the Samantha-ettes (as Nancy calls them) were giggling like maniacs at their table. This was supposed to be a big joke on Tanya, who they thought was a nerd who ate odd foods. She brought "party beets" to my pajama party a while back and Samantha never forgets when somebody does something weird. She makes sure it comes back to haunt them. She and her crowd think making fun of people is extremely witty. Whoever you are, sooner or later the joke is on you.

It's probably going to be on me pretty soon, or else on Nancy, because Samantha can't stand that we saw her in the girls' room during our class dance. She was crying her eyes out because not one boy had asked her to dance. (Several asked *me*.) This time the joke was on her, and there's nothing she hates worse than that.

So now she's both mad at me and Nancy, and

kind of scared of us at the same time. I think she's worried we'll blab what we saw all over school.

I was still feeling pretty good about this tonight after dinner. I was up in my room, supposedly reading for a book report on this biography of three great inventors — Thomas Edison, Alexander Graham Bell, and Samuel Morse. What I was really doing was practicing sticking my nose up in the air in front of my mirror to see how devastating it looked.

But then I was interrupted by voices in the hallway outside my door. My mom's voice, and one I didn't recognize. Not a girl's voice, but not quite a grown-up's either. Somewhere in between. And whoever it was spoke in this lilting way, a little like singing.

"Oh, but your whole house is so, so — how do you say? — homely."

I heard my mother laugh. "I hope you mean 'homey.' 'Homely' means *ugly*."

"Oh, I am so sorry. Still sometimes my expressions are a tiny bit off and it is disaster."

"Don't apologize. I'm impressed with anyone who can speak two languages. You don't even want to *hear* my French. I only learned a little, in high school, and it was terrible even back then."

French! That's when I remembered — tonight was the night Claudine Ferrand was coming by to look at Gram's apartment!

I ran and poked my head into the hallway just in time to see Claudine disappearing up the stairs as she followed my mother. I could only see the back of her. She had the most beautiful long, curly brown hair. Not frizzy like mine is most of the time. Just a perfect tumble of shiny curls. Now there were two things I wanted to trade with her — our names and our hair.

I was dying to see what she looked like, so I waited a minute or two — to look casual — and then followed them up.

"Heat and water are included in the rent," my mother was saying, "but the electricity's on a separate meter from the rest of the house and so you'd need to set up your own account for that."

As soon as I got there, I felt stupid. I mean, I had no real reason for coming up. I just stood, out of breath, in the middle of Gram's little living room. "Uh," I said brilliantly, "I can't find Elvis. I thought he might have run up here."

"Elvis?" Claudine said in her musical voice. "He is another of your children?"

"No," I rushed in to explain. "He is another of our cats. Actually, we only have two now that Gram's cats moved with her. When she married Mr. Bagnold, that is." I suddenly realized that I was babbling. It was because I was trying to talk and at the same time trying to get a good look at Claudine. She was really beautiful — kind of how

I hope I'll look someday if everything goes absolutely perfectly. If I grow about five more inches than it looks like I will. If my hair calms down. If my skin suddenly turns creamy and flawless. If my plain brown eyes get bigger and develop a deep, liquidy look. Of course, to *really* be like Claudine, I'd have to pick up a slight French accent, too, which might be kind of hard around Detroit.

"This is Lizzie," my mom said, kind of introducing us. "She's our middle child, the oldest of our girls."

"Elizabeth," I said quickly. Whenever I meet a new person, I try to get them started on the right foot — calling me Elizabeth. It never works. Within minutes, they're calling me Lizzie. But maybe Claudine was going to be an exception.

"Hello, Elizabeth," she said. "I am pleased to meet you." She had this slightly formal way about her that was nice. And her French accent made everything she said sound better. If she'd handed me a sack of garbage and said, "Elizabeth, please take this out to the trash can," it would've sounded great.

I could tell Claudine was giving the apartment a real once-over. My mom and I waited while she turned on the faucets in the kitchen and looked inside the cabinets. She went through each room twice and turned the switches on and off. She opened the windows and looked at the locks. She was very thorough.

When she was done, she smiled this wide smile that showed her white, white teeth (one of the front ones was turned a little; it was a relief to see she had at least one imperfection) and said, "I think it is absolutely charming. I would love to rent this apartment."

"Wonderful." I could almost hear my mother's sigh of relief. I think she thought Claudine was the perfect tenant (I did, too) and hoped she wouldn't get away.

"When may I move in?" Claudine asked.

"As soon as you like," my mom said. "It's all ready."

"Wednesday, then? My things are in storage and I must call to have them sent over."

"Fine. Why don't you plan to have dinner with us that night? You've already met Darcy downstairs, and Lizzie, and my husband of course. But there are still a few more Milettis you haven't seen yet. Not to mention our pet menagerie. If you come to dinner, you can get the total picture of what life's like around here. Of course, maybe you'd rather *not*."

"No, no. I would very much like to come. I enjoy family life. Especially since I am so far away from those I love. In Paris."

Paris. It sounded so romantic the way she said

it. *Par-ee*. It also sounded so far away. I felt kind of sorry for her. I wondered who all those people were. Her family, of course, but was there a boyfriend, too? Someone she cried herself to sleep over every night? Once in a while I read one of my mother's romance novels and there's always some poor woman crying herself to sleep over some guy (usually a nobleman) who's far away, but close in her thoughts. I can't imagine crying myself to sleep over anyone I know, but then the only guys I know are the boys in my sixth-grade class at Claremont.

"Lizzie?" my mother said. I snapped out of my wandering thoughts, and looked up. Claudine and my mom were standing at the doorway to the apartment, waiting to switch off the light and leave. I blushed at having been caught spacing out. I was glad Claudine couldn't read my thoughts and see I was creating this big life story for her.

I already had about a million questions. How old was she? What was school like in France? What was her favorite subject? Her least favorite? Did she have a best friend back there? Why did she come to the United States? Was she in love with someone she left behind, and if so, why did she leave him? Did she like cats or dogs better? I couldn't very well ask these all at once. I'd just have to wait until she moved in and then slip them in every few sentences or so.

For tonight, all I could do was watch out the window as she pulled out of our driveway in her little red car, and then go call Nancy to give her what few details I had. I had a feeling there was a lot to know about Claudine, and this was only the start.

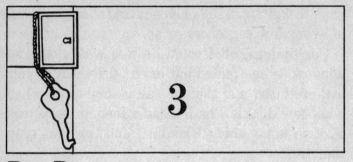

3

Dear **D**iary:

Sorry I haven't written in a couple of days, but so much has been happening. Some of it I wish *weren't* happening. For instance, my history project.

Mr. Burrows got this big idea that none of us in the class were relating to the past. He said we were just looking at history as a bunch of stuff that happened a long time ago. I have to admit this is *exactly* how I see history, but he thinks we need to get involved in it. So we all have to come to class next Tuesday dressed as a person from a particular historical event. We drew slips of paper from a box. Nancy got the French Revolution and she's going as Marie Antoinette — *after* she was beheaded by the guillotine. She's getting one of those Styrofoam heads ladies put their wigs on at night, and painting a face on it, and somehow she thinks we're going to be able to rig her into this black cape of her mother's so her real head is stuck down inside and she'll carry her fake head around.

To shock everyone. If we can pull it off, I have to admit this will be great.

My assignment on the other hand is to come as someone from the Boer War. I'm already behind. I don't even know where Boer is.

So this has me a little depressed. Plus Samantha is up to something weird. I can't put my finger on it, but I thought I detected a strange glint in her eye as Nancy was telling me and Erika Powell about her costume idea. Usually Samantha and her crowd don't lower themselves to associate with any of the rest of us, except to make their withering comments to show how pitiful we all are compared with them.

But as we were all walking out of history class together, Samantha practically tripped over a couple of kids to get to Nancy and offer her a wig.

"My mother wore it to a costume ball once," she said. "It's all done up in these fancy auburn curls, so I think it would look just right for your Marie Antoinette head."

"Uh," Nancy said, stopped in her tracks by Samantha not only speaking to her, but offering to help her out. Finally she managed to add a "Thanks."

"Gee, that was nice of her," Nancy said to me when Samantha had run on ahead into the girls' room. She has to recomb her hair between *every* class.

21

"Yeah," I said. "I wonder what her ulterior motive is?"

"Oh. Well, maybe for once she doesn't have one," Nancy said. "Maybe she's just being nice. I mean, I suppose it *is* possible."

I couldn't believe she was saying this. Nancy, who hates Samantha more than I do. Sometimes she's just so innocent and trusting it kills me. I myself am extremely suspicious of Samantha being nice to anyone out of the blue, but especially suspicious of her being nice to me or Nancy, whom I know she secretly hates. We did, after all, catch her in the most humiliating moment of her life, and I know she hasn't forgotten that. I'm going to have to keep my eye on her like a hawk, to see if this really was just a weak moment of niceness on her part, or the beginning of some sinister plot.

But sinister *how*? I mean, what could she be up to?

I was still brooding about Samantha and her schemes when I got home after school. I was late on account of stopping at Nancy's to listen to a New Kids on the Block tape she'd just bought. Practically my whole family was jammed into the kitchen when I got there, helping Mom get dinner ready for Claudine. Josh and Adam were making one of their Super Special Salads (basically everything from the vegetable bins in the refrigerator).

My mom was baking her great macaroni-and-cheese casserole. Dad was microwaving some "hot dog kebabs." Ordinarily, I would have worried about him pawning off some test product on an unsuspecting guest, but since Claudine worked for Roth Frozen Foods, too, I figured she'd already tasted her share of weird items.

Darcy was setting our big family table in the dining part of the kitchen. Baby Rose was helping her by putting down the napkins. Rose is very particular for a little kid. Everything has to be just so. And so it was taking her forever to line the napkins up just right next to the plates, then to put the knives just right on top of the napkins. In the time it had taken Darcy to set the whole table, Rose had put down two napkins, and now was going back to the first one to straighten it out a little more. I could see from how red Darcy's face was, that Rose was driving her nuts, poking along like that.

"Oh, just let *me* do that!" Darcy finally said, grabbing the rest of the napkins out of Rose's pudgy little hand.

Instantly, Rose started crying, and Darcy had to forget being irritated, and calm Rose down. No one wants to be responsible for making Rose cry. She is incredibly loud, and once she gets on a roll, she can cry forever. I could tell Darcy was upset about more than Rose's persnicketiness. It was all the fuss about Claudine. Darcy was the only one of my siblings who didn't like the idea of Claudine moving in. It wasn't really anything personal. It's just that Darcy had been using the apartment as her playhouse since Gram left and didn't want to give it up.

"I don't want some old lady living in my little house in the sky," she said.

"How *old* is this old lady anyway?" Josh said, slowly tuning in to the conversation.

"Too old for you," I told him bluntly.

"Claudine is twenty-one," my mother said. "She told me the other night."

"I don't think that's too old for me," Josh said, running a hand through his hair as if he were a major star. "You forget I'm extremely mature and sophisticated for a sixteen-year-old. I'm often mistaken on the street for Tom Cruise."

I burst out laughing. "Josh," I said. "To Claudine, you'd seem like a mere child. Stick with Mary Lou Witty. High school girls are more your speed. I'm sure Claudine's boyfriend is someone *really* grown up. Someone suave and continental."

"You some big friend of hers or something?" Josh asked me, raising an eyebrow a little. "You seem to know an awful lot about her."

This made me realize how dumb I sounded. It was true I hardly knew Claudine at all. I'd barely met her. But still, I knew someone like her just *had* to have a wonderful boyfriend who took her to exciting places and made all sorts of great romantic gestures. He would be the kind of boyfriend I'm going to have when I grow up, after I have perfect hair, and an apartment of my own, and no more history projects weighing on my mind.

I couldn't very well say all this to Josh though, and so I had to settle for just giving him my "banana frosty" — the look that kills. I'm very good at giving it.

Just then the doorbell rang and my dad went to bring Claudine into the general chaos of our house. Dinnertime in the loony bin. What would she think of it?

It turned out I didn't have to worry. Claudine loves big, noisy families. She told us this right off. And I don't think she was just saying that, because even when the meal reached its low point, when Rose knocked a carton of milk onto the floor and both cats came slipping and sliding through it before we could begin to get it cleaned up, Claudine saw the humor in the situation.

The whole family seemed to really like Claudine, too. I could tell. Well, it was obvious with Josh, who was practically falling all over himself trying to look cool around her, using every big word he knew, talking about all the reading he was doing, which I knew amounted to two assigned books, and his "upcoming travel plans for hitting the East Coast," which was really his senior trip to Washington, D.C., with about six teachers going along to baby-sit. Everyone else was just normally interested in Claudine, and she seemed really interested in us, too.

She sat at the head of the table — the place we always give guests of honor when we have them. She *looked* like a guest of honor, too. The other time she'd come by to look at the apartment, Claudine had been dressed in what she'd worn at work. High-style in a tailored suit. Tonight, though, she was dressed casually, to move her stuff in. But even her casual look was dressy and formal. Her pants were black and ironed with sharp creases. She had on a black turtleneck, and a vest in a black and pale blue plaid. Black suede boots. Sharp, but not very relaxed looking.

It was the same with her personality. She was incredibly friendly to everyone, interested in what they had to say about themselves. But she had very little to say about herself.

When somebody asked about her family, she said, "Oh, I have a mother and father, and several brothers and sisters." But she didn't say how many, or name them.

When Adam asked what her father did, she said, "Oh, he is in business. What about you? Are you thinking of becoming a businessman?"

"A stockbroker," Adam said. He's the only one of us kids who already knows what he wants to be when he grows up.

"You know this already?!" Claudine said in her accent. "This is so mature for someone your age." Adam got all glowy and blushy at this while Josh looked a little peeved at being passed over in favor of his kid brother.

Claudine's conversation went like that through the whole dinner. Every time someone would ask about her, she'd turn things around into a question about them. I don't think anybody else noticed this, but I did. By the time dinner was over, I felt like Claudine knew a lot about us Milettis, and we still knew hardly anything about her, except that she was from Paris, had gone to college in New York, and that she was working on a big project at Roth that was top secret. I was beginning to feel like everything about Claudine was top secret.

I still had about a million questions to ask her, but when I saw how quiet she was, I knew I probably wasn't going to get information out of her the direct way. If she wasn't telling the names of her brothers and sisters, she for sure wasn't going to tell me if she had a boyfriend and what he was like and what were some of their most romantic moments! I'd have to use trickier tactics.

"I'll help you carry your things upstairs, Claudine," I offered as we were clearing the table. I thought this idea was pretty brilliant. Carrying her stuff up, I'd get to see what records and books she had. A true detective like me can gather a lot of information about a person from these sorts of clues. And then, once we got everything upstairs, I could help her unpack and get even more clues. This plan went down the tubes though, when Claudine very sweetly turned my offer down.

"Oh, thank you, but I really have so little. It is easier to do it myself, I think."

Diary, you are probably going to think I'm crazy, but instead of thinking she was just trying not to be any trouble to us, my first thought — and the thought I'm still thinking sitting up here in bed — is:

She's hiding something. There's something about Claudine that she doesn't want anybody to know!

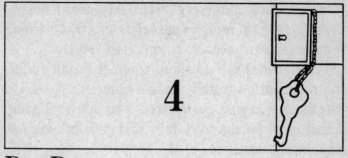

4

Dear **D**iary:

Yesterday I was over at Nancy's house after school. We were supposed to be doing homework together. This is to help Nancy, who is dyslexic and has trouble reading. I'm supposed to be a "study buddy" and general good influence. Instead, I was being a rotten influence, getting her to forget her books and go through fashion magazines to see if we could find a style for long hair that would look good on me. Ever since I'd seen Claudine's hair, I'd decided I wanted mine long, too.

Nancy found a picture she liked, and turned the magazine around and held it up for me to see.

"I don't think so," I told her. "I'd look too much like Cher. Like someone wilder than I really am. People would expect an entirely different personality out of me if I wore my hair like that."

Just then, Nancy's phone rang. (She has an extension right in her room, next to her bed — the height of luxury.)

"Oh," I heard her say. "Hi. Uh, sure. I mean, that's great. I really appreciate it. Okay then, tomorrow after school. Right. See you then."

"Who was that?" I asked, when she didn't offer the information (totally unlike her).

"Oh, it was just Samantha. You know. Saying it was okay for me to stop by and get that wig for my history costume."

"Tomorrow? After school?" I said.

Nancy just looked back at me blankly, totally innocent. "Yeah," she said. "Why?"

"Oh, nothing," I said, hurt. "Only that tomorrow is the day you and I are supposed to meet Gram at the Zephyr for ice cream."

Nancy slapped her forehead. "Oh, boy. How could I forget? Lizzie, I'm sorry. I'm just a total dolt. I'll call Samantha right back and tell her I'll have to do it some other time."

"Oh, don't do that. You really need that wig, and we have to have our costumes ready by next week." (I still hadn't even *thought* about mine. I am a World Champion procrastinator.) "Samantha's so pukey I wouldn't cross her. She might take back the whole offer. I'll just go meet Gram by myself and tell her what happened. She'll understand."

Actually, I had a secret motive in saying this. I wasn't really all that upset that Nancy couldn't come along to the Zephyr. I kind of wanted to have Gram all to myself. But still, I needed to know that Nancy *wanted* to come. For a minute, I thought maybe she preferred going over to Samantha's. This didn't make any sense, given how much Nancy hates Samantha, but you never can tell. Samantha can be very charming when she wants to. She can fool even the smartest people. As I may have mentioned, she even fooled me once. But Nancy is different from me. She's extremely practical. As my mom says, she has "both feet on the ground." She just needed a wig, I told myself, and Samantha was offering one. That was that.

I was still suspicious of Samantha, though. Why was she being so nice to Nancy all of a sudden? That part I couldn't figure out.

By the time I was at the Zephyr, I'd completely forgotten about Nancy and Samantha. I was having too much fun with Gram to think about anything else. We always have our best times at the Zephyr, because we are both ice-cream nuts.

"I could eat ice cream with every meal," Gram told me today as we sat across the sparkly Formica table from each other, digging into our sundaes (hers — raspberry-walnut; mine — peanut butter-marshmallow) "Do you think that's weird?"

31

"Not at all," I said. "But then maybe I'm not the best person to ask. Seeing as I could eat ice cream *as* every meal."

She laughed and tried to try to swipe a spoonful of my sundae. Whatever flavor she orders, Gram always winds up thinking my sundae is better.

"I like your new glasses," I told her, blocking her spoon with mine, like a miniature sword fight. "I've finally decided."

I have to tell you, Diary, that although these glasses are neat, they are also pretty weird. The frames have a kind of tiger stripe pattern in them — very different from the regular, Granny-like glasses that Gram has worn for years. She's been making quite a few changes lately in her style and her life. It's as if, now that she's made this big change of getting married, she's having fun making a bunch of little changes. She's also taking aerobics and has enrolled in a ceramics class.

"Whew!" Gram said, sighing this big, fake sigh of relief as she took off the glasses to look at them again. "I'm so glad to have your seal of approval." She was being funny, but I knew that underneath, she really did care about my opinion. Especially on matters of style. "Do you think they make me look younger?" she asked me.

"I don't know what to say to that because I never think of you as *older*," I told her, and it was the truth. "You're just my friend. I never put an age on you."

"You are such a dear," she said. For a second I thought she was going to cry, but instead, she picked up her spoon and tried to swipe another bite of my sundae.

I was dying to tell Gram about Claudine, which was why I was glad we were alone today. I would have been too embarrassed to talk about this in front of Nancy. She is definitely *not* as interested in the subject of Claudine as I am.

"Claudine this, Claudine that," she said to me yesterday when I was describing what Claudine had worn to work that morning. (Dark blue skirt and sweater, dusty rose coat.) "You just think she's fascinating because she's French."

Which is not true. I think Claudine's fascinating because she's fascinating. Nancy will, too, once she meets her. Even without meeting Claudine, though, Gram was all ears for my description.

"Tell me *all* about your new tenant," she said.

"Well, that's the problem. I hardly know anything about her. She's very mysterious."

I told her about the dinner at our house, and how when anyone asked Claudine a personal question she ducked it. "What do you think she's hiding?"

"Well, she may not be hiding anything," Gram said. "Some people are just very private. Especially at first. And she's new in town. New in this country, really. She might just be shy. Give her a chance to settle in, get comfortable around the house. Don't forget she's facing an awful lot of Milettis at once. I'll bet she opens up in her own good time."

"Maybe," I said. Gram was usually right about people. "I hope so. I have this secret dream that she and I will become friends."

"Well, who could resist that?" Gram said. "Who could not want to be your friend? Especially when they find out how easy it is to snitch ice cream from you." And sure enough, she'd just gotten away with another bite. I made a fast reach for the napkin holder and set it between our dishes like a little barricade, and gave Gram a "This is war!" look. We each held our breath for a second, then both started laughing at once. I love my Gram.

Usually, if we don't walk home from school together, Nancy and I talk on the phone after dinner. But here it is, eight o'clock already. I just (finally!) finished my report on the inventors' book, and looked up at the clock next to my bed and realized I still haven't heard from her about what went on at Samantha the Terrible's house this afternoon. It looks like I'm going to have to call her. In my house, this is not always easy.

Unlike Nancy, we Miletti kids do *not* have our own extensions. To be exact, we have two phones in the whole house. One in the kitchen (forget privacy there), and one in the upstairs hallway. This is the one we siblings usually use. And someone is almost always on it. Getting your own call in edgewise is pretty much of a challenge. But I've just got to find out what happened at Samantha's, so here goes.

I'll get back to you later, Diary.

5

Dear **D**iary:

Me again.

I know it's only about an hour since I last wrote, but my mood has changed completely. Now I'm hurt, angry, and upset. All from making one crummy phone call. To Nancy.

At first, I didn't think I'd even get to make it. When I got out into the hall, the phone wasn't there. I knew this meant someone was probably using it in the hall closet, for privacy. I followed the cord and opened the door and sure enough, there was Josh, all scrunched up on the floor having one of his sickening conversations with Mary Lou Witty. At least these conversations are sickening on Josh's end. I never hear what Mary Lou is saying. What Josh says is practically nothing. He just sits there holding the receiver so close to his mouth it looks like he's about to swallow it. My opinion is that if a person is going to say nothing, they don't have to hog the phone to do it.

"Come on," I said, but Josh just waved me away as though I were an irritatingly buzzing fly. (Since he has turned sixteen, Josh looks at the rest of us siblings a lot as though we're irritatingly buzzing flies.)

I went downstairs and got a glass of milk and came back up. I opened the closet door and this time *Adam* was inside — with his boom box! Which meant he was playing one of his dumb rap songs over the phone to his friend Eric. Another monumental waste of phone time.

The next time I tried the closet it was even worse. Darcy was inside having one of her stupid arguments with her friend Jennifer. All these arguments are pretty much the same and go like this.

"No, I don't," Darcy says.

Jennifer says something I can't hear.

"Yes, you do," Darcy says.

Jennifer makes some brilliant comeback I can't hear.

"I do so," Darcy says.

If I listen any longer than this, I begin to go crazy.

This time I stood outside the closet door, tapping my foot until Darcy got off. I was afraid if I left and came back I'd find Baby Rose on the phone to someone from her play group.

Finally, when it was almost nine o'clock, I got a chance to call Nancy.

"So how'd it go?" I asked.

"How'd what go?"

"Your visit to the Imperial Palace of Her Royal Highness Samantha."

As you know, Diary, in addition to being beautiful, Samantha is also rich. She not only has her own phone — she has her own number! Plus a TV and VCR in her room. Plus more outfits than Nancy and I have put together. Plus, when our family spends a measly week in a rented cottage on Harsen's Island in the summer, Samantha's parents are taking her off to Switzerland or someplace like that for three months. Even if you hate Samantha, you still can't help envying her.

"Did she let you swim in her indoor pool?" I teased Nancy. So far as I knew, this was one thing Samantha didn't have.

"Actually, we went waterskiing on her indoor lake," Nancy teased back.

"Come on. Really. What happened?" I just knew Nancy would have some great piece of gossip about Samantha and we could spend a little while dishing her. And so you can imagine my surprise when she said, "Well, it was kind of fun."

"Fun *how*?!" I said.

"Well, for one thing, I didn't know Samantha

was into bird-watching. She has some really good books — field guides to Latin American birds, even one on Australian species."

Nancy is a bird-watching maniac. It's one of the few interests we don't share. It just seems like a waste of time to me, frankly, standing in the middle of the woods with a pair of binoculars pressed to your eyeballs, waiting hours for some blue-tipped thrush or something to sit on a branch for a minute so you can mark off that you've seen one.

Nancy's never been able to get anyone interested in bird-watching with her. It's not exactly a "hot" hobby, if you know what I mean. Which means it's for sure not the sort of thing Samantha Howard, who likes to think she's about the coolest person in the universe, would ever let herself be caught doing in a million years. I tried to subtly point this out to Nancy.

"Funny," I said. "I don't recall Samantha being a big bird-watcher."

"Oh, she's just gotten into it recently. I was a little surprised myself. It doesn't seem like her cup of tea, but I guess bird-watching is just so much fun it interests all sorts of people.

I was trapped. I couldn't say I thought Samantha's sudden interest in bird-watching sounded pretty phony to me, because Nancy might take this as an insult to one of her favorite things in life.

All I could say was, "Well, that's great. You've found someone who loves the little chirpers. Too bad it's Samantha, a person you can't stand to be with for more than ten seconds."

"Oh, I don't know," Nancy said. "She might not be as bad if you got her away from that dumb crowd of hers."

"Right," I said, my voice dripping with sarcasm. "Samantha's only problem is that she's been hanging out with a bad crowd. She's really a peach at heart, a wonderful person— practically Mother Teresa."

"You don't have to be sarcastic, Lizzie." There was a hurt tone in her voice.

"But I *do*. I have to remind you that we are talking about Samantha Howard, who, in all the years we've known her, has never shown a good side. She started out in preschool, knocking over our castles in the sandbox, and has just kept on being awful ever since. She's a rotten egg. A bad apple. To the core."

"I'm not so sure about that," Nancy said. "I think maybe she's changing now."

"Nancy, a leopard never changes its spots. You're making a big mistake to trust her."

"I'm not trusting her," Nancy said huffily. "I'm just going bird-watching with her."

"You are? When?"

"Sunday afternoon."

"You didn't tell me that."

"You haven't given me a chance."

What was going on here? First, Samantha all of a sudden helping Nancy with her costume. Now developing this big interest in Nancy's hobby. Something was definitely fishy. I didn't say anything, though. I *couldn't* say anything. I couldn't tell Nancy who to be friends with. It was her choice. Even if I felt she was making a big mistake, I had to keep my mouth shut or else sound like I was a jealous friend. Which I guess I am.

Nancy right away tried to change the subject — to my Boer War costume, but it was too depressing to even think about on top of everything else. I just said I was already working on it (a total lie) and didn't need any help. And then I pretended that someone else wanted to use the phone and so I had to get off.

As it turned out, someone *was* waiting to use the phone when I opened the closet door — Baby Rose!

She was standing in her favorite fuzzy purple pajamas, rubbing her eyes. Her cheeks were all red and wet, so I knew she'd been crying.

"Did you have a nightmare?" I asked her.

She nodded. "I was going to call Brooke from my play group and tell her about it."

I think she was still half asleep. For sure her little friend Brooke would be *sound* asleep.

"Tell me about it instead," I said, taking her by her little hand back to the room she shares with Darcy. "Sisters are better than friends. They're truer blue."

6

Dear **D**iary:

I've become a spy! I don't quite know how this happened. It all started out very innocently.

This afternoon Mom came in from shopping at the mall. She was carrying this big, square cardboard box.

"What's that?" I asked, as I held the back door open for her so she could get inside with it.

"I bought a bedside lamp for Claudine. Gram took her reading light with her when she left and so I had to find something to replace it." When we got it out of the box and unwrapped it, the lamp was much smaller than the box — just a little, pink ceramic table lamp.

"Would you mind taking it upstairs?" Mom said, sitting down on the sofa and pulling off her shoes. "I've been running around that mall all morning. I feel like I've been in a marathon."

"No problem," I said, practically leaping at the chance. "Is Claudine home now do you think?"

Mom shook her head. "She went shopping. I don't think she's back yet."

Ever since she'd come to dinner on Wednesday, Claudine had been nice, but distant. That is, if I ran into her, she was usually dashing upstairs on her way in, or downstairs on her way out, and just gave me a little wave and a laugh and said hi. My plan to make friends with her was going nowhere. She seemed like this terrific person I was never going to get to know, even though she was living in my very own house.

At first I felt disappointed that she probably wasn't going to be upstairs when I brought her lamp. The lamp would have been a good excuse to get into her apartment, and then hang out awhile and talk. But then I thought again and realized that Claudine being gone would have its advantages, too. I could have a look around. I wasn't planning to snoop exactly, just to be super-observant while I was walking through with the lamp. I am very good at this. As I may have told you, I think I'd make a great detective.

I knocked on the door at the top of the stairs, but as I expected, there was no answer from the other side, and so I turned the knob and pushed the door open.

I looked around in surprise. The place looked quite a bit different from when Gram lived there. All the posters of Impressionist paintings were gone from the walls, replaced by posters of scenes of Paris with French names on them. And where Gram had had her stereo equipment and records, there was a small bookcase filled with CDs.

I didn't figure there was anything sneaky about just looking over someone's collection of music, and so I went through the discs. Mostly they were country music. I thought this was a little weird for a French person, but maybe she liked America and thought country was *really* American.

On the shelves below the discs, there were books. I went through these, too. I don't think this was snooping either. I mean if anyone wanted to look over the books on my shelf, I'd let them. Although if they tried to look at *this* book, at you, Diary, I'd have a fit. Most of Claudine's books were in French, so I couldn't tell what they were about. She also had a few American novels, and this self-help book called *How to Meet Guys*. Maybe she didn't have a boyfriend after all. Maybe she was looking for one.

After I'd gone through the books, it just seemed natural to go and look around in the kitchen. By this time, I was kind of imagining myself as a real detective, a sleuth like Sherlock Holmes, trying to put together the puzzle pieces of the mystery — the mystery in this case being Claudine.

Her kitchen cabinets were filled with the sort of things eaten by a person living alone. Soup for

One. Cans of tuna. Packets of Ramen noodles. Inside the refrigerator, things were a little more interesting. There was a small carton of milk and one onion in the vegetable bin, but also there was a bottle of champagne in the door and a wedge of French cheese on one of the shelves. These seemed like exactly the sorts of things I could imagine Claudine serving when her boyfriend came by for a date.

It was about then that I realized this was what I was looking for, evidence that Claudine had a boyfriend, and a wonderfully romantic life with him. The funny thing was that, for all my snooping, it turned out I could have found this evidence just by doing exactly what my mom had asked me to do in the first place. Because when I finally brought the lamp into the bedroom and went to put it on the nightstand, there was my proof, right under my nose!

Inside a heavy, fancy silver frame was a color photo of a guy, a very good-looking guy, with a motor scooter propped against his hip. He was smiling slyly at the camera, and in the background was the Eiffel Tower. Even I, who have been practically nowhere, know the Eiffel Tower when I see it. I knew that meant the picture had been taken in Paris. But even if there hadn't been such a big clue in the photo, I would have known this was no guy from around *here*.

Everything about him was different. His hair. It was short on the sides, but fell in a long wave over his forehead. His pants were tight black jeans and his sweater was baggy and a wonderful shade of plum. And he was wearing the tiniest pair of sunglasses. Maybe I'm not getting the point across, Diary, but this guy was *really* cute!

Across the lower right-hand corner of the picture was an inscription, written in big, heavy letters, like this:

Toujours amour.
Laurent

Toujours amour. Laurent. That had to be his name. Laurent. Like Laurence or Larry, only French. *Amour* meant "love." Even though I don't know any French, I knew that. I didn't have a clue about *toujours* though. I'd have to ask my mom. She took French in high school.

Thinking about my mom startled me into realizing that it had been some time since she'd sent me up with the lamp. She might be wondering where I was. Or worse, Claudine might come home and walk in and find me holding her boyfriend's photo, trying to figure out the inscription.

47

I put it back on the nightstand as though it were a hot potato, and scooted out of the apartment and down the stairs to my own room.

I sat on the edge of my bed for about three seconds. That was about as long as I could stand to hold this new piece of information without telling Nancy. I ran downstairs and pulled on a sweatshirt and headed out the back way.

"I'm going to Nancy's!" I called to my mom, who was reading a story to Rose, who was almost asleep on her lap. I was out the door before I remembered what I wanted to ask Mom. I ducked my head back in.

"What does *toujours* mean in French?"

"Always," my mom said distractedly. "Why?"

I couldn't very well say "Oh, I was snooping like crazy up in Claudine's apartment, and I found this picture of her boyfriend and was just trying to make out the extremely personal inscription at the bottom." So I had to make up one of my terrible lies.

"Oh," I said, "I'm doing a book report on Madame Curie and in this one part she says '*toujours* science!' So I guess it means 'always science.' It was probably her motto."

Thank goodness my mother has five kids and doesn't concentrate too hard on any one of us. That's the only possible explanation for why I can get my terrible lies past her.

48

Always, I thought as I walked over to Nancy's house. *Toujours* meant "always." Which meant that Claudine's boyfriend had written, "Love always" on his photo. How romantic, I thought, and sighed. I couldn't wait to tell Nancy.

She was up in her room, sitting cross-legged on her bed, looking through this huge book of bird pictures, which I just knew in my heart of hearts Samantha had given her. I thought maybe she was going to be too absorbed in birds to care about my great detective work. But even more than being a bird-watcher, Nancy's a nosey person.

When I told her what I'd found in Claudine's apartment, her eyes lit up. She closed the bird book and whistled this low whistle and said, "I want to see it, too."

This shook me up a little. "I don't know," I told her. "I mean I had this excuse for going up there today. But how would we get up there again? And when? What if we get caught? At least if Claudine had come back this afternoon, I could have explained I was dropping off the lamp." Suddenly I didn't feel so much like a person in a houndstooth jacket and double-billed cap like Sherlock Holmes. I didn't feel like a great detective. I felt like a prying little snoop poking around in somebody else's business. Nancy teased me.

"Oh Lizzie, you're not going to chicken out just

when this is getting good. I don't want to keep *hearing* how cute the French guy is. I want to see for myself."

"Okay, okay," I said, starting to be sorry I'd told her. "I'll think of *some* way to get you up there."

"I already know how," she said. "I'll sleep over tonight. If Claudine goes out, up we go. You can stand guard and I'll be the spy this time. We'll work out a plan. It'll be foolproof. Don't worry about a thing."

But I *am* worried, Diary. What have I gotten myself into? I don't want to seem like a wimp in front of Nancy. But I'm nervous that we're going to get caught, and get in trouble with Mom and Dad, and worse, with Claudine.

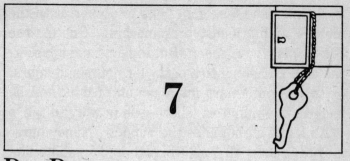

7

Dear **D**iary:

Last night (Saturday) Nancy came to my house to sleep over. I was nervous about her coming because I knew that she was going to insist on spying in Claudine's apartment to get a look at the picture of Laurent. I'd gotten away with snooping around up there once, but I didn't want to press my luck. A little voice inside me said, *Don't do it!* And I always try to listen to my little voice, because it's usually right.

Maybe Claudine would stay in for the night. Then we wouldn't be able to go upstairs. About seven, just when I was expecting Nancy to arrive, I heard the side door slam and looked out my bedroom window to see Claudine leaving. She wasn't at all dressed up — just jeans, but skinny designer jeans. As I've said, Claudine is always kind of dressed up, even when she's dressed down. She got into her little red car, warmed it up for a minute, then puttered off down our street.

If she'd been dressed up, I could have been

fairly sure she was going out to dinner or to the movies with friends, or something. Out for the *evening* is what I mean. But in jeans and a jacket, she could be going to a party for hours and hours, *or* to the mini-mart for a carton of milk and be back in five minutes. There was no way to tell.

As I was standing at the window, Nancy burst into my room, all out of breath and smelling like outdoors. She pulled a flashlight out of her jacket pocket.

"I thought this might come in handy in our detective work," she said, giving me a little punch on the arm. "I just saw Claudine drive off in the Claudinemobile. So the coast is clear, as they say."

"I guess," I said gloomily. Then I noticed something different about Nancy. Something about her hair. It was a different style than it usually is, which is no-style. Nancy is pretty much wash-and-wear when it comes to her hair. Once, a little while back, she got a perm, but it was a disaster and since then she's gone back to her basic "no style at all" look. In the summer she just smashes her hair underneath a baseball cap. Sometimes she washes it before she goes to bed and sleeps on it all night, then shows up at school with one side matted to the side of her head, the other sticking straight out. This doesn't bother her at all. You could probably give her a crew cut in her sleep and she wouldn't mind.

Basically she thinks style is for dorks like Samantha and her crowd, girls who want to seem grown up. "Pseudo-teens" Nancy calls them. She, on the other hand, wants to stay a kid as long as she possibly can.

"What's the rush?" she says. "I'm supposed to get all excited about being a teenager? So I can wear nail polish and get zits and fall in love with one of the incredibly exciting boys in our class. Wow." She says this in her most sarcastic voice.

This attitude was one of the most frustrating things about Nancy. I'm not in that big a hurry to grow up myself, but I don't want to be a stick-in-the-mud like Nancy, either. I don't want to spend the rest of my life riding my bike and doing history homework and eating peanut-butter-and-banana sandwiches and acting as though the boys in our class were either invisible or totally gross. Actually, some of them are starting to seem better to me, more like regular human beings and less like creatures from another planet. Billy Watts for one. He's the boy I danced with the most times at the school dance. I can actually talk to him like a friend.

Nancy and I argued whenever we talked about this subject of growing up. I'd just about given up. Which is why I was surprised last night to see that she'd gone off on her own and done something neat to her long blonde hair, putting in these zig-

53

zaggy little waves down one side. She sat down on the opposite end of the bed from me and I leaned forward to get a better look.

"What's this?" I said, lifting up a zigzaggy strand.

"Oh," she said casually, "Samantha lent me her crimper the other day. She thought it might give me a hot effect. I was just fooling around with it this afternoon."

Samantha lent Nancy her crimper?! Nancy was styling her hair because Samantha was her beauty adviser?! I couldn't believe what I was hearing. I'm sure my eyes were bugging out.

"Do you like it?" she asked me, running her fingers through her crimps with this flippy, ultra-feminine little gesture I'd never see her use before.

I did like it, but since she'd gotten the idea (*and* the crimper) from Samantha, I didn't want to show that I did.

"It's okay," I said. I could tell Nancy was nervous about her new look, and I should have been nice about it, but I was just too jealous. I hated like poison that she and Samantha were becoming friends. At first I'd just been worried that Samantha was up to her usual tricks, but now I was less sure. Maybe she really liked Nancy and really wanted to be her friend. Maybe they'd find they had so much in common that they would become *best* friends, and I'd be shut out. I just couldn't stand the thought. I didn't know what I'd do without Nancy for a best friend. The thought was too sad to even think it.

"Are you still going bird-watching with Samantha tomorrow?" I asked.

"Yeah," she said. "You know, I'm beginning to think Samantha's not as bad as we thought. I think she's really only snobby when she's with Candace and Jessica. I think they might be bad influences on her. When she's by herself, she's really a lot different."

"What are you saying?" I almost shouted at her. "Samantha Howard is *not* different when she's alone. She's always exactly the same. She's rotten to the core."

"Well, I'm just not sure of that anymore is all I'm saying," Nancy said. "Give me a break, Lizzie. I'm just going bird-watching with her. It's no big deal. And it's not until tomorrow. We've got more important things to think about tonight." She pointed upwards, toward the attic.

But just then we heard my dad's booming voice.

"Lizzie! Nancy! Come on *down!*" He liked to impersonate the emcees on TV game shows.

"What's up, do you think?" Nancy said to me. "Big Fun?" She knows my dad well enough to know that when he has that tone in his voice, he has what he calls "Big Fun" in mind — some adventure or expedition for all the family, or as many of us as he can round up.

"Let's go see," I said and we both hopped off the bed and ran downstairs.

Down in the family room were my dad, my mother, Adam, Darcy, and Baby Rose. Josh was out with Mary Lou Witty.

"What's up?" I asked my dad.

"I called up the Bowlarium and it's Family Night," he said. "I figure we qualify." Then he took Nancy by the arm and told her. "Just keep quiet and we can pass you off as our niece from Idaho."

As if the Bowlarium checked to make sure you were a true family on Family Night. Sometimes my dad's pretty funny.

"You want to go?" I asked Nancy. I was relieved when she nodded "yes" excitedly. I figured this meant we'd be out for the evening, which would cancel out our plans to sneak up to Claudine's apartment.

So I put that problem out of my mind the whole time we were at the Bowlarium. It was a great night. I am usually a terrible bowler. Being little and skinny, I can never get enough power to really hurl the ball down the alley. But this time I just concentrated hard and aimed carefully, and so even though the ball rolled along at the most ex-cruciatingly slow speed, it wound up knocking over quite a few pins. Once I even got a strike! My highest score of the three games we bowled was 121, which isn't great, but it was great for me and I was happy.

By the time we got home, it was almost ten and I was sleepy. Nancy seemed wide awake, though. She'd bowled really well, one game she got 142 and was really up about it. She wanted to go over her highlight moments.

"Maybe I should think about becoming a professional bowler," she said as I took my shoes and socks off, and pulled out my sleep T-shirt. "Oh," she added, "you're not getting ready for bed, are you?"

"Why not? You've got another idea?"

"I thought you were going to take me . . ." She didn't finish her sentence, just pointed toward the ceiling.

"Nancy! It's way too late for that. Claudine's probably back by now."

Nancy shook her head. "I looked for her car when we came back. It wasn't there."

"Oh, Nance, come on. She could come back any minute now. It's just way too risky."

Nancy nodded. "I thought you'd say that. It's like Samantha was saying the other day about you. How you always like to play it safe."

"What?! She said that? What did she mean?"

"Well, I think she meant stuff just like this.

Here's a situation with an eentsy-weentsy risk factor and you're shaking like a leaf and backing out. This is one case where I'd have to say Samantha might be right." As she talked, she pretended to be inspecting her nails, not looking at me.

All of a sudden I felt my ears get hot, that's how mad I was. Just the *thought* of Samantha talking to Nancy about me, saying I'm a wimp, or a lily-livered chicken or whatever she actually said (I both wanted to know, and didn't want to) made my blood boil. It was like in those old swashbuckler movies where one swashbuckler slaps the other with a glove and the slapped guy just has to pull out his sword. I felt like I was being challenged, not only by Nancy, but by her new "friend" Samantha. I couldn't sit still for that.

"All right, what are you waiting for?" I said to Nancy.

"What do you mean?" she said.

"I mean if you want to go up to Claudine's, let's do it now. Come on." I tried to look totally nonchalant as I led the way out of the room.

I tried not to let Nancy see how nervous I was as we made our way up the stairs to the attic. When we got to the top, I turned and put a finger to my lips to signal her to keep very quiet while I pressed my ear to the door, just in case Claudine had parked around the corner or something and was already home.

But I didn't hear anything from the other side. And when I got down on the floor to look under the door, I didn't see any light from the other side. I didn't want to do this, but unless I went ahead with it, Nancy and Samantha would just have proof that I was a wimp.

I turned the door knob slowly and pushed the door open. The apartment was totally dark. The only noise was the humming of the refrigerator in the kitchen. I flipped on the light switch by the door. Immediately I felt Nancy's hand on mine, shutting it back off.

"No," she whispered. "If she drives up, she'll see the light. Let's just use this." She switched on her flashlight and aimed it at the floor in front of us as we walked in. "Now," she said, turning back to me. "Where's this picture?"

I nodded toward the bedroom, and she led the way. She saw the photo right away and trained the beam of the flashlight on it.

"There," I said, trying not to sound like the nervous wreck I actually was, "now you've seen it. Let's get out of here."

"Lizzie," she said, looking at me with pity. "You are such a nervous jervous. I want to see it up close." She walked on ahead of me and went to the nightstand and picked up the framed photo and pointed the flashlight straight at it. "You're right," she said. "He *is* cute. If there were boys like this at Claremont, I might change my opinion about the species."

Then we heard it, both of us at the same exact instant. The click of heels followed by the slam of the side door.

"It could just be Josh," I said. Everyone else was already in for the night.

Nancy shook her head. "Josh only wears running shoes. They don't click. It's Claudine for sure."

"Let's run for it then," I said.

She shook her head again. After accusing me of being a nervous jervous, now *she* was the one with panic in her eyes. "Too late. If she's already in the house, we'll run into her just as she's heading down the hall to get to her stairs. We've got to hide."

"But where?!" I squealed.

Nancy slapped her hand over my mouth. "Quiet. Calm down," she said. "Think. Is there a storage closet or something up here in the apartment? Someplace she wouldn't look late at night?"

"There's a pantry off the kitchen," I said.

"Let's go then!" she said as we heard the door at the bottom of the stairs open. "Tiptoe," Nancy said, shining the light in front of us as we ran as fast as we could on tiptoe.

We made it to the pantry at almost the exact same moment we heard the knob of the apartment door turn and then heard Claudine's footsteps come into the living room. I slowly shut the pantry door so that it didn't make a click.

Nancy turned off the flashlight as we both stood there facing each other — staring, but not seeing anything, our eyes not yet adjusted to the sudden darkness.

What were we going to do now? How were we ever going to get out of this mess?

8

Dear **D**iary:

Saturday night continued:

Adam came in before, and I didn't want him to see me writing. If he knew I had a diary, he'd be snooping all over this room to get his paws on it. So I put you under my pillow and distracted him by taking him downstairs to make some popcorn. Now I'm back and can finish telling you about last night.

First, for a long time, we stood silent and rigid as posts while Claudine came into the apartment and rustled around. I guess she was taking off her jacket. And then we heard her shoes drop. One. Two. We relaxed a little when she went into the bedroom. Nancy tugged at the sleeve of my sweat-shirt to signal me to sit down on the floor of the pantry with her. By this time our eyes were ac-customed to the dark and we could see each other pretty well. She pointed to the keyhole in the door, and we took turns kneeling so we could look through it.

Not that we could see all that much unless Claudine happened to walk by the entrance to the kitchen. It's really weird, trying to figure out what somebody's doing just from listening to them through a closed door and what little you can see through a keyhole.

For a while, Claudine was in the bathroom. We could hear the swooshing sounds of her brushing her teeth. The next time she came by the kitchen I could see she was wearing just a T-shirt and underwear, which is exactly what I wear to bed. It was kind of neat seeing that Claudine and I had something in common.

"She's getting ready for bed," Nancy whispered to me. "As soon as she's asleep, we can sneak back out, and downstairs again."

"Are you crazy?!" I hissed into her ear. I couldn't imagine sneaking out while Claudine was in the apartment. Of course, I couldn't imagine staying in the pantry all night either.

We sat together in silence for a while, listening for Claudine, but not really hearing anything. Then all of a sudden I had a terrible thought, and felt a shudder pass through me involuntarily.

"What?" Nancy said.

"I just remembered. Gram used to have a problem with mice in her pantry."

"Mice?!" Nancy started to scream, but I was fast enough to cover her mouth with my hand before she could even get the "m" out.

"Shhhh," I said to her, in what I hoped was my most calming voice. "I'm sure she got rid of them. Actually, now that I remember, I'm positive she did."

This was a total lie. I wasn't at all sure Gram had gotten rid of her mice. She has such a soft heart that she hates to set the kind of traps that kill the mice. But at the same time, she's so frightened of mice she can't bear to use those traps that just catch them so you can let them go again in the backyard. What she wound up doing basically was ignoring the mice. Which probably meant they were still living in the walls of the pantry. I didn't mention this to Nancy though, and just hoped none of them would come out tonight. If that happened, we'd both probably scream and bolt out and give ourselves away to Claudine, who would be more frightened to see us than we'd been to see the mice.

We could hear her rustling around again. I started to tense up. "Don't worry," Nancy said, reading my mind. "She won't come in the kitchen."

Practically the second she'd finished saying this, the overhead kitchen light came on and the two of us jumped into each other's arms out of fright.

"She's going to come in the pantry!" I whispered into Nancy's ear.

"Why? So she can get a midnight potato? Get real." Still, just to be on the safe side, we stood up as quietly as we could and flattened ourselves against the walls of the pantry away from the door.

Luckily, Claudine didn't come into the pantry. She just got a soda out of the refrigerator. I could tell that's what she was doing because I could hear the pop of the top followed by that fizzy sound. She didn't have a chance to stay in the kitchen longer because just then her phone rang. Nancy and I gave each other the same surprised look. Who could be calling her so late?

"Laurent!" I whispered, cupping my hand around Nancy's ear.

"Hello?" we heard Claudine say when she'd run into the living room and picked up the receiver. (When she says "hello?" it actually sounds more like "allo?")

Of course we couldn't hear what was being said by whoever was on the other end of the line, but we could tell *a lot* from what Claudine said.

First she laughed her musical little laugh. Then she said, "Why are you calling me so late? Aren't you worried you will wake me?" You could tell she was teasing when she said this though. I just knew it was Laurent, calling all the way from France.

"You are such a funny person," she told him. "I thought you were funny all night."

"   " he said.

"You see. A very funny person. Quite peculiar. I'm not sure why I like you so much."

"   " Whatever he said made her laugh again.

"Yes, well you *do* have a few good character traits, I'll admit."

"   "

"You are? Well, that's sweet of you to say."

"   "

"Me? Well maybe. Maybe a little. Maybe a lot." I couldn't tell exactly what they were talking about, but for sure it was love talk. Which meant it *had* to be Laurent. I felt a kind of thrill rush through me just thinking of how romantic it was of him to call all the way from Paris in the middle of the night. I tried to figure out what time it was for him, but I'm no good at that. I can never remember where it's earlier than us and where it's later and where the International Dateline is and what Greenwich Mean Time really means. We learned all that just last year, but already it's hazy in my mind. Plus I didn't want to stop to figure out time differences and miss out on any of the juicy parts of the conversation.

It didn't go on much longer though, and the rest of it was more of the same — goofy romantic talk. Which I just hate when I hear Josh doing it on the phone with Mary Lou Witty, but for some reason was furiously interested in hearing now that it was Claudine's conversation. Even her good-bye to Laurent was so soft and romantic I almost blushed to hear it.

And then I peeked through the keyhole to see Claudine flop onto the couch with this dreamy look in her eyes. She stayed there just like that, not sleeping, but not moving off the couch either. And then she put on a country music record and danced around a little by herself. I sometimes do this when no one's around, but I didn't know anyone else danced by themselves.

Finally, after what seemed like hours, Claudine got up, turned out the lights, and went into the bedroom. Nancy and I waited for another long time, until we were as sure as we could possibly be that Claudine had fallen asleep. We stood stock still, pressing our ears against the door of the pantry. It was then, in the darkness and stillness that I felt it. Something brushing against my ankle. I knew it wasn't my imagination. It was a mouse!

I felt a scream fill my throat, but I stifled it. If I screamed, Nancy would, too, and Claudine would hear and our goose would be cooked. She'd be furious and I would have lost any chance of her ever being my friend.

Then, it happened again. Why hadn't I put my shoes and socks back on before we came up here? This time I could almost feel every mouse hair and mouse whisker as they tickled my skin. I thought for sure I was going to faint. But I didn't. I just steeled my mind and whispered to Nancy, "We can probably leave now."

I turned the knob on the pantry door as slowly as I could. It squeaked what was probably only a little but, in the silence of the apartment, it sounded like a huge screech. We waited. Nothing.

We stepped out of the pantry on tiptoe. Luckily we were both barefoot so our steps didn't make any noise on the linoleum floor of the kitchen. I led and Nancy followed close behind. I went slowly so I wouldn't bump into anything or knock anything over. Actually, our eyes were so accustomed to the dark and there was so much moonlight coming through the skylight window in the living room that I could find my way easily.

Our last hurdle was the front door to the apartment. I couldn't remember if it squeaked or not. I tugged gently at the handle, hoping I'd hear nothing but silence. Instead, there was a long squeak of the door on its hinges.

I held my breath and could feel Nancy holding hers behind me. From inside the bedroom, Claudine muttered something in French that I couldn't understand.

We waited. More silence.

"Talking in her sleep," Nancy whispered. "Let's get going before she wakes up."

We slipped out the door and pulled it quickly shut behind us with another squeak, then took the stairs two at a time until we were back in the hallway by my room. We collapsed against the wall, first heaving this huge sigh of relief, then at the exact same second, burst out laughing.

My mother must've heard us because she opened the door to her bedroom and peered out blearily, "Lizzie?"

"It's just me and Nancy," I said. "We got hungry. We're going downstairs for a snack."

"Oh. Okay," she said and started to close the door, then opened it again and looked at me in this way she has when I can tell she doesn't quite believe what I'm saying, but doesn't have enough evidence to accuse me of anything specific.

Since I'd told my mother we were going for a snack, that's just what we did. While I rooted around in the cupboards for some cereal, Nancy and I talked about our adventure, and how we almost got caught, and I told her about the mouse. At first she didn't believe me. She didn't think I could be that brave. But I finally convinced her it really had happened. Then I said, "The whole thing was the scariest I've ever done, but I think I'd do it all over again. Just to have gotten to listen to Claudine's phone call. I mean it was so romantic. Wouldn't you just love to have a boyfriend like Laurent?"

"I might," she said. "But apparently Claudine wouldn't."

"What do you mean?" I asked her. I had no idea what she meant.

"Lizzie. Wake up. She was speaking English. If she were talking to her French boyfriend calling all the way from France, don't you think she'd speak French to him? Don't you think they'd speak in their native language, especially since it's supposed to be the universal language of love?"

"I still don't get what you're saying," I said. "You mean she's peculiar for speaking English to Laurent?"

"I'm saying I don't think she was *talking* to Laurent. I think she was talking to someone else. Probably someone here. Probably whoever she was out with tonight."

"How can you know that?"

"She said she thought he was funny all night. Do you think she thought Laurent was being funny in Paris? I don't think so. Our Claudine, I'm afraid, is a two-timer."

"What's that?"

"Someone who has two boyfriends at once."

"No," I said, refusing to believe it.

"You're just saying that because you like her so much you don't want it to be true. But when you think about it, it's the only logical explanation. She's keeping poor Laurent on the string over there in France while she's dating some guy here in Hampton Point."

"I don't believe it!" I said, getting angry.

"Don't then," Nancy said. "I know I'm right. You wait and see."

Oh, Diary, I hope Nancy's wrong. I just can't believe anyone as nice as Claudine would do something so rotten. I need to prove to Nancy that she's wrong. And I *will* prove it. I only need evidence. But to get it, I'm afraid I may have to do a little more detective work.

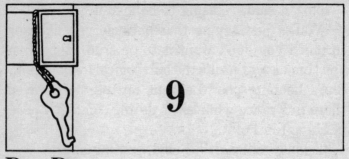

9

Dear **D**iary:

It's Sunday night, and I'm so sad I don't know if I can tell you what's happened since I last wrote.

I got up at the crack of dawn this morning. This is very unusual. On weekends, when I don't have to be up for school, I like to sleep in as late as possible. But this morning, I must have heard a bird outside my window because I woke up thinking *Today's the day Nancy's going bird-watching with Samantha.* And then I rolled over and burrowed under the covers to go back to sleep. Instead, my eyes popped wide open as I sat up in bed remembering something Samantha had said. It was a couple of weeks ago. She and her friends were sitting at the next table over from me and Nancy in the lunchroom and I heard her say, "I am the laziest pig on weekends. I never get up before noon. I'm like a bear in my cave. Heaven help anyone who tries to disturb me."

This was the *same* Samantha who was going to meet Nancy over at the bird sanctuary this morning. I looked at the clock next to my bed. It wasn't even eight o'clock yet. Something fishy was definitely going on. Why would Samantha change her whole personality and body clock just to go bird-watching with Nancy? What was she plotting?

But then I had another thought. A worse one. What if she *wasn't* plotting anything? What if she just liked Nancy so much that she was willing to change her ways so she could be a good friend? But if she liked Nancy *that* much, if she really wanted her for a friend *that* much, she probably wanted her for a *best* friend.

Then I felt this terrible sinking sensation. If Samantha wanted Nancy for her best friend, I could never compete. Samantha has everything to offer. She even has a pool in her backyard. Last summer, Candace Quinn got to go to London with Samantha for a week. They all saw plays and ate fish and chips and the two of them talked about it around school for most of September. Maybe next September it would be Nancy and Samantha talking about their trip to India to see the Taj Mahal. They'd be laughing together at the lunch table and passing around photos of the two of them riding elephants. I really got going on this nightmare fantasy. By the time I got to the part about the elephant riding, I was so upset there was no way I could get back to sleep. So there I was, the first one in the house awake at eight on a perfect sleep-in Sunday morning. I might as well be out bird-watching with Nancy. With Nancy and her new best friend, Samantha.

Actually, I wasn't quite the first creature stirring around the house. Sebastian must've heard me tossing and turning because pretty soon he was pulling off my covers to show me it was time to get up and take him outside.

"Oh, all right," I said and put on my sweatpants and wound up not only taking the dog out, but helping my dad (the next human to wake up) make pancakes for the whole family.

Then I did all my homework except history, which as you know, I hate. I still hadn't done anything about my costume. I made a note in my looseleaf binder. *Costume*. I'd look up the Boer War the next day in the school library. I knew I was down to the wire.

I took Sebastian for a long walk to the park in the afternoon, and stopped by Nancy's house on my way home. Her mother answered the door. "Nancy's not back yet," she said.

"She must be finding some incredible birds to be gone this long," I said, trying to sound as though I wasn't all that concerned. But Mrs. Underpeace knows me pretty well and I could tell my voice was quavering, so I was probably a dead giveaway.

"Oh, they're back from the bird sanctuary. She

74

called and said Samantha's parents were taking them up to Aldridge, horseback riding."

Horseback riding?! I thought. Nancy loves to ride horses. I do, too, but we hardly ever get to go. Sometimes, if Mrs. Underpeace is in an incredibly good mood, she'll take us up to the stables at Aldridge. If we can't get up to Aldridge, Nancy loves horses so much she'll just go on the pony rides at Kiddieland. (Sometimes she is just totally embarrassing.)

What I started wondering then was just how did Samantha know horseback riding would be the absolutely most tempting offer to make to Nancy?

I was crushed. I'd just assumed Nancy and I would hang out together this afternoon, like we do most Sunday afternoons. I felt like I was going to cry, and I was embarrassed Nancy's mother would see me blubbering if I stood there much longer. I wish I didn't cry so easily. It's mostly a curse. Wearing my heart on my sleeve, as my mom says. Everybody knows just what I'm feeling, usually just when I'd rather they didn't.

I looked away and muttered, "Well, tell Nancy I was looking for her. Nothing important. I was just out walking Mr. S. and thought I'd stop by." Then I just turned and walked off as quickly as I could.

I felt so dejected all the way home. There I was, walking my dog, alone on a crisp, sunny Sun-

75

day afternoon while my best friend was off having
Big Fun with Samantha Howard. It wasn't that
I didn't want Nancy to have other friends. Lots
of times she and Ericka Powell did stuff together.
But usually it was stuff they'd asked me to come
along for, but I couldn't. I knew if Samantha Howard were in the picture, I'd *never* be asked along.

Samantha likes to swoop down on new friends
and throw a fence around them. PROPERTY OF
SAMANTHA HOWARD. Even in her own crowd, she
plays Jessica and Candace off against each other.
She's friends with one, then with the other.

Now she was swooping down on Nancy — for
whatever reasons. And I knew Nancy was liking
it. I knew she was enjoying the attention of the
oldest, prettiest, most sophisticated girl in the
class.

But how was Samantha going to use her? To
get what? Deep down I knew there was something
rotten underneath all of Samantha's niceness to
Nancy. Even though I think Nancy's the greatest,
I just knew that wasn't why Samantha was trying
to be friends with her. Because Samantha could
never do anything for that simple a reason. That's
just how she is.

Nancy didn't call tonight, either, like she usually does. And I didn't call her. It felt like a point
of pride that *she* call *me*.

I knew there could be a million reasons for her not calling. She might have just been ultra-busy with her homework, since reading takes her an extra-long time. Or it could have been that her mom, who can be kind of strict sometimes, had put her foot down and told Nancy, "No more socializing today."

But in my heart of hearts I took that un-called call to be a sign of the end of our friendship. And the beginning of the new best friends — Nancy and Samantha.

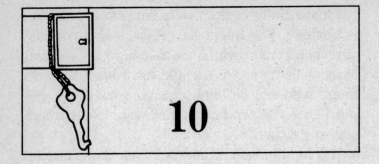

10

Dear **D**iary:

It's Monday night and I'm sitting up here on the bed in my little blue room with a jumble of feelings going around inside me like tennis shoes in a dryer.

I'm feeling sad about Nancy. We didn't ride to school together, because her bike was broken. She was nice enough to me in school, but a little far-off. When I saw her at our lockers (they're side-by-side) in the morning, she was wearing a pink sweater I didn't recognize. We both have so few outfits we know all of them by heart. This was definitely a new sweater. Maybe her mom got it for her. My guess, though, was that Samantha had lent it to her. It had a Samantha look about it.

"I'm sorry I didn't get to talk to you last night," Nancy said to me. "I got back kind of late and my mom went into Prison Warden Mode. You know, 'Do your homework. Help me sort the laundry.'

Then, when I finally got a chance to call, your line was busy."

Ordinarily this would've been a perfectly good excuse. Our line is *always* busy. Today, though, I felt myself not quite believing her.

Nancy had to see her reading tutor during lunch period, so I sat with Ericka Powell, and wound up telling her the whole story about Samantha and Nancy.

"Maybe I'm crazy," I told her when I was done. "Maybe I'm just making up this weird fantasy in my head."

But Ericka shook her head and said, "Nope, Samantha's up to no good for sure."

"How do you know? Because of your deep intuition? Your keen insights on people?"

"No. Because I overheard Samantha telling Candace on the field trip to the conservatory the other day."

"Telling her what?"

"That she was going to drive a wedge into your and Nancy's friendship. I didn't want to say anything to you, and get you all bent out of shape. I thought maybe she'd forget and go on to some other victim, but it looks like she hasn't. But why do you think she'd want to do that to you two? For *what* reason?"

Suddenly everything was clear. Samantha was trying to get back at me and Nancy for seeing her crying in the girls' room at the class dance. She'd been humiliated in front of us, and this was her way of paying us back for seeing her at her lowest moment. She was going to make friends with Nancy to ruin our friendship and once she'd done that, she'd drop Nancy like a hot potato.

"Boy, I haven't a clue why she'd want to do that," I lied. Even though I hated Samantha and even though she was being her most rotten self to me, I still wouldn't snitch on her. That would make me an equally rotten person.

"Well, what are you going to do about it?" Ericka asked me.

"I don't know," I admitted. "You have any suggestions?"

"Put her in a box with air holes and ship it somewhere far away."

Even in the middle of being sad and mad, I had to crack up at that picture.

After school, I finally got to the school library and looked up the Boer War. I was really surprised. I thought it happened in the Stone Age or something, but it was really a war around the turn of this century. In Africa. It was fought between the English and the Dutch. There were no pictures along with the encyclopedia entry. I thought of trying to get away with just wearing a monocle and a top hat to pretend I was English. Or wooden shoes to pretend I was Dutch, but somehow I knew Mr. Burrows wouldn't let me get away with something like this.

I went up and asked Ms. Johnson, our librarian, if she had a book on outfits worn in the Boer War. Ms. Johnson is very young, and really funny, but in a sarcastic way. I always forget this and always get snagged by her sense of humor.

This time she looked at me with real wide eyes and said, "Oh, sure. Actually we have a sixteen-volume set on uniforms of the Boer War."

At first I thought she was being sincere, and I really brightened up. But then she said, "Get real, Lizzie. You'll be lucky if you find one mangy picture. Is this for that class project of Burrows?"

I nodded.

Ms. Johnson sighed this big sigh like someone in a play sighing, and got up from her chair behind the librarian's desk. "You know, they teach us in library school to try to keep the books on the shelves, away from the kids, but in your case I'll make an exception."

I followed her into the stacks. As we walked, she turned around and asked me, "You want to be English or Dutch?"

"English, I guess," I said. "Well, whatever's easier."

"Probably English," she said and pulled down this big old book.

"*A Pictorial History of England,*" I said, reading the title as she set it down on one of the old tables in the library and opened it. In just a few minutes, she'd found what I needed — a drawing of a soldier wearing khaki jodhpurs and high boots and a khaki shirt with a belt across his chest and medals over his heart. On his head he was wearing a pretty strange hat.

"What do you call this?" I asked Ms. Johnson.

"It's sort of a pith helmet. You know, like African explorers wear. But it's shaped like an English bobby's helmet."

"What's a bobby?"

"A policeman," she said, then added, "boy, they should pay me extra for giving out information like this."

"I'm going to look like a mail carrier in the summer," I moaned. "I'm going to look stupid."

"Not as stupid as Billy Watts," Ms. Johnson said.

"Why?" I asked. "What's his historical event?"

"The Bubonic Plague."

Somehow this cheered me up a little.

When I got home, my mind was on where I was going to get the parts of my costume, so I almost passed by the mail sitting on the little table in the hall. Actually, I was past the table when the picture on the postcard struck me and I went back.

I looked down at the stack of bills and all the other uninteresting kinds of mail our family gets and checked out the postcard on top. I recognized the sight in the picture. It was the Arc de Triomphe. We learned about it in geography last year. It's in Paris. Which meant this card had to be for Claudine.

I bent way over. I was already deep in my detective mindset. If Claudine was suspicious that somebody in the house was snooping on her, if she'd woken up the other night and heard her door shut, then this postcard might very well be a trap. In mystery novels, people are always setting traps like this. Setting out something desirable and then rigging it so they'll know if someone has looked at it. Usually this rig is a fine thread of hair placed carefully across the item in question. Something the ordinary person wouldn't notice, and so would knock off when he picked the item up. I looked so closely I probably looked like a nut case bending over there, but I couldn't see any hair or thread. It was probably safe to pick up the card.

As I suspected, it was signed in the same heavy script as the photo. Above it was scrawled, "I am missing you so much and think about our family and about looking at you again. I am practicing my English for coming over there. How is it, do you think?"

Oh, it was awful, Diary. I mean, I could barely stand to think of this incredible guy pining away over there for his true love Claudine, if Nancy was right and Claudine was also in love with someone else — someone here in Hampton Point!

But she *couldn't* be. I read the card again. He was thinking about "our family." Clearly that meant they'd talked about getting married and having babies. That meant the relationship had to be a serious one. *Very* serious. No one in such a serious relationship with one person would also be dating another person. Especially not anybody as nice as Claudine.

I put the thought out of my mind entirely and didn't even have a chance to wonder about Claudine for the rest of the night, I was so frantic trying to get my costume together. Khaki jodhpurs were the easy part. I had some khaki pants and could just stuff them into the tops of my winter boots. I thought the shirt would be a snap, too. I mean I figured that between my two brothers and my mom, the only other people in our house whose clothes I can kind of fit into, one of them would own a khaki shirt. But no luck. No luck on the pith helmet either until Darcy of all people came to my rescue and suggested we make one out of papier-mâché. She is the papier-mâché wizard of the third grade. Even so, it took us a couple of hours and looked a little more like a dome than a hat, but it would have to do. It was getting late and I still had to deal with the matter of the shirt.

I had an old white blouse, which would probably do if I could dye it khaki. Of course, by this time it was about ten at night and we didn't have any dye. Then I was passing by the Mr. Coffee in the kitchen, which still had the dregs of my dad's morning coffee sitting in its glass pot, and I had the brilliant idea of using it as my dye. It worked pretty well, too. I poured the coffee in the bathroom sink and kept dunking the old blouse in it until it was close to the shade of my pants. Then I didn't rinse it out or anything. I didn't want to lose any of the color, so I just hung it on a hanger on the shower pole.

Then I rigged up a couple of my dad's belts so one would go around my waist, the other diagonally across my chest. Then I cut some little pieces of colored wrapping ribbon to make "medals."

When I was done with all this, I felt incredibly accomplished. Usually this happens. Once I finally get around to a project, I do a pretty great last-minute job and am sorry I didn't start on it sooner and do a *really* great job.

I was beat by the time I got ready for bed. I turned out my light and was just glancing out the window on my way across the room and into bed. A car I didn't recognize pulled into the driveway and sat there for a few seconds with its engine running. Two people were inside. They were just shadow figures from so far away, but I could tell they were very close to each other. *Very* close. And then I saw them lean in toward each other and I knew they were kissing.

At first I thought it was probably Josh and Mary Lou Witty. I know she has her driver's license. Maybe it was her mom's car. But then the door on the passenger side opened and who came quickly out, shutting the door behind her and then standing in the driveway watching as the car backed out and drove off? I don't think I even have to tell you, Diary.

It was Claudine.

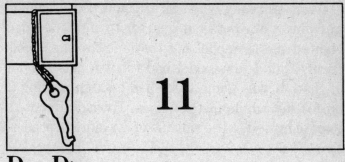

11

Dear **D**iary:

Tuesday.

Nancy called in the morning and said her mom would give us a ride over to school with our history costumes. I was happy about this, both because it meant I wouldn't have to lug my Boer War suit over there myself, and it indicated she was still my friend in spite of being under Samantha's spell.

I'd though about telling her what Ericka Powell had told me. About Samantha trying to break up our friendship, but I decided against it. She might not believe me, and then she'd just be all huffy, thinking I was acting like a jealous friend who didn't want her to have fun with anyone else. Or else she'd confront Samantha, who would wriggle out of it with some excuse. Samantha's great at acting. They could give her the Academy Award for some of her performances.

No, I was just going to have to keep my mouth shut on the subject — for now at least.

* * *

I was all ready when Mrs. Underpeace honked in front of our house at quarter to eight. My dad wanted me to model my costume for the whole family, but I just said I had to rush and got out of that. It was going to be bad enough putting it on for my whole history class. I wasn't about to expose myself to the ridicule of my older brothers, too.

Nancy and I squeezed into the backseat together. In addition to my books and lunch, I had my pants and boots and my coffee-dyed shirt and my medals and belts and my knee socks and my papier-mâché pith helmet, more accurately known as "the flying-saucer hat."

I was traveling light compared to Nancy, though. She had her mom's long cape, which we were going to rig over her head. Her real head, that is. Her severed head was inside a big plastic garbage bag so no one would see it until the perfect moment.

We giggled all the way to school, about our costumes and what Mr. Burrows would think of them, and what Billy Watts would look like dressed as the Bubonic Plague.

I was also dying to tell her about what I'd seen the night before in my driveway. But I couldn't, not with Mrs. Underpeace sitting right there in the driver's seat. Claudine and her mysterious life were a secret between me and Nancy.

I had to wait until lunchtime to talk with her again. I hung around the door to the lunchroom. Nancy took forever getting there. I wound up eating half my sandwich out of the bag just standing there. Finally she came toddling down the hall.

"Hurry!" I said, grabbing her arm and practically pulling her into the cafeteria.

"Why? Are they serving liver today?" Sometimes Nancy can be pretty witty.

"I've got something *big* to tell you," I said.

"What?"

I looked around. We were in the middle of a million kids. "Not yet."

She looked around, too. "Are there spies in here?" she teased me. "I've heard the Claremont lunchroom is a notorious hangout for KGB and CIA agents. Not to mention James Bond."

"Nancy, please," I said. "I just want a little privacy." I found it at an empty table off to the side.

"Well?" Nancy said as she pulled a cupcake out of her lunch bag. Nancy always eats her dessert first.

"Claudine has a boyfriend. Here in Hampton Point. I saw them kissing in his car last night."

"Ask me if I'm surprised," Nancy said, patting her mouth as if she were yawning with boredom at this information, which she already knew.

"I know you suspected it," I said, "but I didn't believe it. Now, though, I must admit the evidence seems pretty overwhelming. What are we going to do?"

"What do you mean?" she said, starting in on her egg-salad sandwich. "Why do *we* have to do anything?"

"For Laurent's sake," I said. "He loves her so much. And everything about him — the way he looks, his handwriting . . ." I stopped to tell her all about the postcard. "He just seems so totally wonderful, so perfect for Claudine. I think she's just been temporarily distracted by this guy here. I think we could do something to make her see the light, drop him, and go back to Laurent. I don't think it's too late. *If* we move fast."

"What do you have in mind?"

"I'm not sure," I admitted. "Talk to her, *if* she'll let us."

"But we don't ever talk to her. You hardly even *see* her, and she lives in your house!"

"We'll ask her to do something fun with us. Something real American. We know she loves anything American."

"We could go to a country concert in Detroit," Nancy said. "But I don't think I could stand it. I hate country music."

"I know!" I said, a bright idea lighting up in my

head. "We can ask her if she wants to go roller skating with us."

"Are you sure roller skating's American?"

I had to admit I wasn't sure. "No harm asking her anyway," I said, and Nancy agreed.

"But even if we've got her on wheels and having a great time, do you think that's enough to get her to confide in us?"

"I'm not sure about that either. But we can steer the conversation to boys and boyfriends and boyfriend problems."

"A subject on which we're positive experts, seeing as neither of us has ever had a boyfriend."

"So we'll make some up," I said. "We'll sound like such experts, she'll be dying to spill the beans on us."

Nancy crumpled her lunch bag and shook her head. "I don't know. Maybe it'll work. We can give it a try."

I have to say Nancy did not seem as enthusiastic about the idea as I was. I think ordinarily she would have been. Her mind was somewhere else. Probably on the next fun thing Samantha had planned for them. I could tell how much fun she was having with Samantha just by how little she was talking to me about it. Ordinarily she tells me everything. Of course, ordinarily we both hate Samantha. Things had changed though, and even

91

if Samantha did drop Nancy like a hot potato, by the time that happened we might be so far away from each other that we wouldn't be able to get close again.

And Samantha would have won.

This thought made me incredibly sad, but I couldn't think of anything to do about the situation. Maybe if I talked to someone wise. Maybe if I talked to Gram.

I didn't have a chance to think about the problem with Nancy any more because from lunch on, all anybody in Mr. Burrows's history class was thinking about was the "Pageant of Time" as he was calling this costume event.

"Samantha drew the Building of the Pyramids," Nancy informed me on our way out of the lunch room.

"She'll come as Cleopatra," I guessed.

"How did you know?"

"Because Samantha Howard always has all the luck. She would never have drawn the Bubonic Plague, or the Discovery of the Wheel. She'd never have to come in a shaggy animal skin, or impersonating a disease. Samantha would only ever pick the little slip that said 'Building of the Pyramids' on it so she could come in a beautiful costume, outdoing everyone else."

"No, my dear," Nancy said as she whirled off

into her English class, "*I* am going to outdo everyone else. If I don't lose my *head* about it."

And she was right. Nancy was the hit of the
pageant. I helped her on with her cape in the girls'
room, then handed her her head and led her
through the hall into Mr. Burrows's classroom.
Everyone else was already there so we made a
big entrance. Hardly anyone looked at me, my
costume was so boring. All eyes were on Nancy
as she came into the room walking like Doom it-
self, carrying her severed head (she'd done a
really good job of painting "blood" around the
neck) and saying in this grim voice from inside
the cape. "Let them eat cake!"

It was a great effect. Everyone loved it. Some
of the kids even applauded. Mr. Burrows exploded
with this big, hearty laugh. He really is a very
nice guy if you overlook the fact that he's a history
teacher.

After a little while, Nancy just wore the cape
the regular way and went around with two heads
for the rest of the hour.

Samantha looked gorgeous, as I predicted. Billy
Watts won hands down for the grossest costume.
His bubonic plague victim had a tattered costume
of rags and these giant wads of bubble gum all
over his face to show he had the plague. Plus he
walked around the room groaning. None of the

girls would even go near him. Sometimes sixth-grade boys simply do not seem mature enough to be considered in the same category as sixth-grade girls. I tried to imagine what Samantha would have done if she *had* drawn the Bubonic Plague. Somehow she would have made it look glamorously tragic or something. For sure she would not have come with bubble gum on her face.

A couple of kids came up and said they thought my costume was good, but I knew they were just being polite. My costume was boring. Nobody could even guess what I was supposed to be. Ericka Powell, who'd come as "The Boston Tea Party" with a tri-cornered hat and a rubber axe and a crate marked TEA, guessed that I was the explorer Stanley who came to Africa looking for Dr. Livingstone.

"Close," I said. "It's the hat that's misleading. I'm actually a soldier in the Boer War."

"Is somebody making coffee in here?" she said, looking around.

Then Tanya Malone came up to me. She'd goofed on her assignment, which was the Discovery of America, and came as a pilgrim instead of Christopher Columbus. "Are you supposed to be the first U.P.S. delivery person?" she asked me. Anyone else, I'd think they were being sarcastic, but Tanya was so out of it, I figured she was probably being sincere. I explained who I really was while she started sniffing the air before asking me, "Do you smell coffee?"

Then Mr. Burrows got everyone to sit down so we could all give our presentations, which was the easy part. And then he surprised us all by wheeling in an audiovisual cart from the hallway, only on it was a big chocolate cake and a bowl of punch. Which turned the pageant from a class assignment into a party. I had to admit the whole thing had turned out to be more fun than I'd expected. No one rushed off when the bell rang. They just hung around having fun with history.

After a while I started to itch and figured it was the coffee in the shirt. I went to get Nancy, who was enjoying being the center of attention, I could tell. I figured she'd be about ready to go home, though. We usually walk together. Sometimes she still rides her bike to school, but even on those days, she'll usually walk it home to talk to me.

"You about ready?" I asked, coming up and tugging on her cape.

She nodded, but then all of a sudden Cleopatra was swooping down on us.

"Oh, Nancy," Samantha said. "You haven't forgotten — you know . . ."

The "you know" was meant for me, I could tell. To shut me out of whatever their big plans were.

Nancy wasn't going along with this, though.

She might be falling under Samantha's spell, but she was still my friend, and a basically good person. So she turned to me and said, "Oh, Lizzie, I forgot Samantha wanted to go to the Zephyr after school." Then she turned to Samantha and said, "I'm sure you won't mind if Lizzie comes along."

But Samantha *did* mind.

"Well, of course I wouldn't mind," was how she put it, "but Candace and Jessica are coming, too. That makes four. Just enough to fill a booth. If Lizzie comes, I'm afraid she'll have to sit by herself in another booth. I don't think that would be much fun for her."

She said all this to Nancy, as if I wasn't there.

Nancy turned to me and shrugged, "I'm sorry, Lizzie. I forgot I told Samantha I'd go with them."

"No, it's okay," I told her, and I meant it. If she'd already made plans, she should keep them. It didn't really matter to me if she went to the Zephyr without me. What was making me sad was something bigger — that if Nancy was going to start hanging out with Samantha and her friends, I wouldn't be able to just automatically count on her being there to do things with me. I'd have to start calling before I just dropped by her house. I'd have to make plans with her days ahead. Things wouldn't be the same old easy way between us that I'd always counted on.

As I watched Marie Antoinette and her head,

and her friend Cleopatra walking down the front steps of school together, I felt tears start to run down my cheeks.

I needed help, and I knew where to turn. I'd go see Gram.

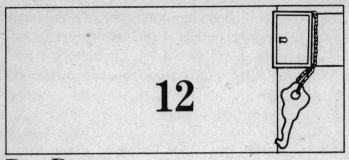

12

Dear **D**iary:

Wednesday night.

I went over to Gram's straight from school. I went around the back way and saw her through her kitchen window. She was wearing her green golf sweater (golf's the new hobby she's taken up with Ralph) and her tiger glasses.

I could see she was deeply absorbed in something. When I got to the back door, I could see she was reading a cookbook she had open on the counter. Next to the cookbook, sitting there like two little loaves, were her cats, Trouble and Mischief.

Gram had a flour smudge on her nose and a million cans and jars and spice bottles and flour sacks open around her and a big bowl in front of her. She was clearly up to some serious baking. I'd come at the right time!

I tapped on the windowpane in the door. I just wanted to signal her that I was there, but I guess she'd been concentrating so deeply that I startled her. When she heard the tap, she jumped back from the counter, and the cats, following her cue, hopped off the counter in opposite directions.

Then she saw it was me and pressed her hand to her heart and came over to open the door for me. I pantomimed "I'm sorry" through the glass, then repeated my apology as soon as I was inside the kitchen. "I didn't mean to scare you."

"Oh, I guess I was just absorbed in trying to figure out this darn recipe." She handed me the cookbook. I closed it and looked at the cover.

"Desserts for Good Health," I read aloud. Under the title were photos of awful-looking desserts — cakes that looked like bricks, pie wedges that could double as doorstops, and lots of bags and bottles of healthy-looking ingredients. "I didn't think desserts were supposed to be healthy," I said. "I thought they were just supposed to be delicious."

"Well, Ralph's doctor told him this marriage is ruining his health. He's put on weight and his blood pressure and cholesterol levels are up. He's got to eat less and more sensibly and exercise more. That's where he is now, at the gym. But he says he simply can't give up my baking. So I'm trying to streamline it. This is my first attempt." She pointed to the recipe she was following.

" 'Good for You Peanut Butter Cookies,' " I read.

"They've got oat bran and whole grain flour and safflower oil and blackstrap molasses instead of sugar. Wheat berries. Organic peanut butter instead of the processed kind."

"They look awful," I said, looking at the photo above the recipe. "They look like those rawhide chew disks we give Sebastian."

"They do, don't they?" Gram admitted. "Well, maybe they'll taste better than they look. Only one way to find out." She pushed up the sleeves on her golf sweater and pushed her tiger glasses up to the bridge of her nose.

"Uh," I said, "mind if I keep you company while you bake?"

She looked up at me and smiled. "Lizzie. You know there's nothing I enjoy more than your company. If anything, I wish you'd stop by more often. Since I've gotten married, I don't feel I see enough of you. I don't know what's going on in your day-to-day life."

"Oh, not much," I said, not wanting to start off the conversation whining about my problems. But Gram knows me too well. She could hear in my voice that something was wrong. She looked up from her cookbook and straight into my eyes.

"Want to tell me about it?" she said as she began to sift the beige flour into the big bowl.

"Oh, it's just about me and Nancy . . . and Samantha."

"What's Samantha doing in that sentence? I thought she and Nancy were like oil and water."

"They were until a couple of weeks ago when Samantha decided they were going to be best friends." I explained the whole, awful series of events. Gram nodded and listened hard, even though she was also mixing her cookie batter and setting the oven to warm up and then dropping the cookie batter onto the greased cookie sheet. By the time the cookies were in the oven, I'd told the whole horrible story in all its gory details.

"So?" I asked Gram as she rinsed her hands and wiped them off on the towel stuck in the refrigerator door handle. "What can I do? How can I stop Samantha from taking my best friend away from me?"

"By not letting her," Gram said. "If you're right and this is all a big scheme of hers, you are the necessary ingredient to make it work. If you don't rise to the bait, she can't win. If you're not mad about her and Nancy being friends, she hasn't succeeded in destroying your friendship."

"But it's so hard not to mind. They've been doing everything together. What if it's not a scheme and she really wants to be Nancy's best friend?"

"Well, that would be another problem. But you don't really think that's what's going on here?"

"No."

"Well, if it's too hard *not* giving Samantha what she wants, you could try giving her *exactly* what she wants."

"I don't get it. What do you mean?"

"Well, you could get Nancy to try a small experiment with you. Stage a big fight, someplace everyone would be sure to see and hear you. Then don't speak to each other for a few days. If you're right, Samantha will think she's won, and she'll drop Nancy like a hot potato and Nancy will see it's all been a scheme."

"But how will I get Nancy to go along with this?"

"That I can't tell you. Grandmothers don't know everything."

She was pulling the cookies out of the oven. She slid them onto a plate and then poured us each a tall glass of milk.

We waited, looking at the cookies as they cooled off. When it looked like they wouldn't burn the insides of our mouths, we each picked up one and took a test bite, and chewed. And chewed. And chewed.

Finally Gram asked me, "Well, what do you think?"

I took a sip of milk and then told her honestly, "It tastes like a slightly peanuty hockey puck."

Gram's mouth grew into a smile, which then

burst into a laugh. Which made me laugh, too. Through her tears of laughter, she said, "Oh. Poor Ralph!"

When I got home, Mom was in a state of total frustration. I think being a mother of five gets to her sometimes. She was wrestling with Baby Rose when I came into the bathroom, trying to get her to sit still so she could give her some medicine. Rose had an earache, which was making her crabby.

"Lizzie," my mom said, turning toward the doorway where I was standing, "could you take out the trash? Neither of the boys is here, and the pickup's tomorrow morning."

"Sure," I said, even though taking out the trash is my least favorite chore.

I went downstairs and dragged the giant plastic sack out the back door and hauled it out to the alley, pulling my jacket tight around me to fight against the wind, which was blustering around. When I opened the big bin where we put our trash, it turned out to be overstuffed with papers, which started flying out in all directions, dancing on the gusts of wind.

I raced around, trying to grab them all up. When I looked at what I was holding, it was mostly torn pieces of a beautiful, heavy, blue-gray stationery. I looked at the writing on one of the pieces and recognized it instantly. It was Laurent's!

I could make out the words, but since it was only a scrap, I couldn't really get the sense of what he was saying.

miss y

desperate to s

All the sentences stopped where the paper had been ripped.

I sorted through the papers in my hand and found three more pieces of the same paper. Then I looked around frantically and saw a couple more pieces blowing up against the McAdams' garage behind me. I ran and got them, and then went back to the bin, where I found two more. I stuffed all the pieces into my jacket pocket and ran inside. I'd piece them together once I got up to my room.

But then, on my way upstairs, who should I run into in the hall but Claudine, on her way out. I was so nervous I nearly fainted. What if she saw Laurent's stationery sticking out of my pocket? I put my hand in just to make sure this didn't happen. I wanted to say a quick hello and bolt, but this was my perfect chance to ask her to go roller skating with me and Nancy and I didn't want to pass it up.

I was amazed when she said sure right off the bat.

"I am so pleased you are asking me, Elizabeth," she said and smiled. "I don't have so many friends here in Hampton Point yet."

Friends! She thought we were friends! She wasn't acting at all like she thought I was an eleven-year-old twerp. She was acting like it was the most normal thing in the world for us to go out and do something together. I could have given her a giant hug right then and there, but:

a) I'm too shy

and

b) I thought maybe French people don't give hugs.

So I settled for just grinning like an idiot and suggesting we go on Friday, since we wouldn't have school or work the next day. She said that would be fine, and I grinned some more, then said good night and went into my room, trying to walk casually so it wouldn't look too much like I was dying to get away from her so I could piece together a piece of her extremely personal mail I'd just stolen. I was progressing from being a snoop to practically being a criminal, but I didn't care. There was no way I could *not* read this letter.

When I was in my room, I shut the door tight and pulled all the pieces out of my pocket. I began laying them out on the top of my desk, like a jigsaw puzzle. In a few minutes, I had everything in the right place, but also could see that there were several pieces missing. I'd have to make sense out of Laurent's letter from what I had.

Claudine,
I will practice my English ag–things here are–without y–I know you must stay–your work–but it–difficult for me alone here–falling apart–very depressed–love toujours–L

I didn't really need all the pieces to understand the message. Clearly Laurent was sinking without her and was trying to ask her, without asking, to come back to Paris. I felt awful for him. There he was pining away like crazy while Claudine was here in Hampton Point, being misled by this mystery guy. Whoever he was, I just knew he couldn't possibly be as wonderful as Laurent, or as right for Claudine.

I took little pieces of tape and hinged the letter together so I could show Nancy at school tomorrow. I'm keeping it under my pillow with you, Diary, so no prying Miletti eyes chance upon it. What would any of my family say if they found out how I've been spying on Claudine? I don't want to think about it. I've got too much on my mind already.

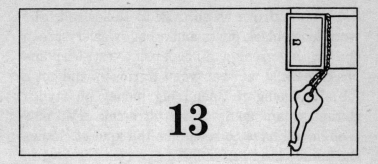

13

Dear **D**iary:

When I showed Nancy the taped-up letter from Laurent, she agreed that the situation looked bad for him.

"At least we're going to get a chance to try to talk with Claudine about this." I told her about asking Claudine to go roller skating. I expected her to be all excited, but instead she said, "Friday? Uh-oh."

"What do you mean?" It wasn't like Nancy to have a big social schedule or anything.

"Well, the thing is, Samantha is having a party at her house Friday night. She asked if I'd come."

"Oh, Nance, you can go over to Samantha's anytime. But we're just not going to have that many opportunities to go out with Claudine. But suit yourself." I tried to sound like I didn't care, but inside I was hurt until she called back a couple of hours later, and said she'd come.

* * *

Claudine drove us all over to Rollerland. She wore loose black pants and a baggy celery-green shirt with a green-and-black print vest. Claudine has convinced me that when I grow up and get a job, I'm going to spend big money on stylish clothes. I am going to be ultra-chic. For now though, I'll have to settle for the kind of clothes the middle kid in a family of five gets. As I sat in the passenger seat, I tugged at my old red sweater and gray sweatpants a little to make them seem baggier, more unstructured. It was the best I could do.

I was kind of nervous in the car with Claudine on the way over to pick up Nancy. It wasn't anything she did or said. It was just that I felt funny. I mean there she was, thinking we were new friends getting acquainted, while all this time I'd been sneaking around in her apartment and hiding in her pantry and reading her mail. She didn't know this, but I did, and it set me on edge.

I lost the nervous feeling by the time we got Nancy and pulled into the parking lot of the roller rink. Friday was the perfect night to be there because there was a mix of adults and kids. There were as many people there around her age, and even much older, as there were kids like us.

Claudine admitted she'd never been on roller skates before. Nancy and I aren't that great shakes ourselves, so we all just sort of clung to each other as we slid around the floor like a trio of old men on an icy day. I'm sure we were pretty funny to look at. We didn't care. We were laughing too hard at ourselves to be embarrassed by anyone else laughing, too.

We skated through fast songs and disco numbers and slow tunes with rotating colored lights dancing all over the walls and ceilings. After a while, Nancy started getting brave and skating off by herself. Once, just clowning around, she tried to imitate this really good girl we'd been watching skating backwards. Of course, when Nancy tried this, she got about three feet before she fell smack on what Claudine politely referred to as Nancy's *derrière*.

Finally, when we were out of breath, we skated over to the railing and clomped through the opening to the snack bar, where Claudine said she'd treat us all to Cokes and hot dogs.

It was easy to talk to her. She wanted to know everything about us — what Claremont was like, what our best subjects were, our favorite rock stars. We were talking for quite a while before it dawned on me that Claudine was doing the same thing she'd done at my house at dinner that night. She was finding out a lot about us, but not telling us much about herself in return. I decided some direct questions might be necessary to get the ball rolling in that direction.

I asked if she was enjoying it in Hampton Point, or if she was homesick.

"Oh," she said, laughing, but in a sad way, Diary, if you know what I mean, "I think a little of both. I am liking it here very much. The job. Other things. I am also sorry not to be at home, though. There is a problem I should be taking care of, and from this distance, I cannot so well."

"What kind of problem?" I said, prying, but I didn't care.

"Oh," Claudine said, as if I was prying, "it is, I think, a little too painful just now to talk about." Clearly though, she was talking about things with Laurent.

"Have you made any friends here in Hampton Point?" Nancy jumped in. Not too subtle, I thought, but maybe it would do the trick. Maybe she'd admit she made a terrible mistake, and ask our help in undoing it. But she didn't say anything about it.

"Oh, well, I guess you could say I was lonely here at first, but . . ." and then she paused such a long time I thought maybe she wasn't going to finish her sentence. But she finally did, saying, ". . . but not anymore."

Nancy and I sat there with open mouths, waiting for more, for details on *why* Claudine wasn't lonely anymore. *Who* was the person making her

110

not lonely? But there were no more details. Instead of continuing the conversation, Claudine just popped the last bite of her hot dog into her mouth, crumpled up her little paper napkin and waxed paper into a ball, smiled, and said, "So? We go back to skating? I am having so much fun I hate to stop."

And that was that — end of conversation, end to any more clues about Claudine's secret life. We couldn't talk while we skated. Most of the time we were laughing too hard. And on the way home, Nancy mentioned her Marie Antoinette costume, which Claudine thought was hilarious. Then she wanted to know everything about the "Pageant of Time." What everyone's costumes were and all. We were still talking about this when we pulled up at Nancy's.

I told Claudine she could just let us both off there. I was sleeping over. "So we can talk through the night," Nancy explained.

What she didn't say was that most of the talking we'd be doing that night was about Claudine herself. "Boy that was fun!" Nancy said, shooshing around her room backwards, as if she were still skating.

"Yeah," I agreed, "but we didn't find out as much about Claudine as I hoped we would. Still, we did get some new info. We know she's unhappy about leaving Laurent behind. And that this romance she's gotten into here is just the result of her loneliness when she first came to town."

"Wow!" Nancy said, flopping onto her bed next to me, rolling over, propping her head up on her hand, and looking at me wide-eyed. "How'd you get that much out of the few things she said?"

"Astute listening and keen observation," I said. "Trust me. I know I'm right. Claudine is stuck. She doesn't know what to do. She's still in love with Laurent, but now there's this guy here. He was nice to her when she first got to Hampton Point, and now she doesn't have the heart to tell him she belongs to someone else. Someone wonderful back home. Nance, we've just got to help her out of this mess."

"But how?"

"I don't know. I'll have to think about it."

"Are you sure she's going to want our help?"

"Well," I said, a little nervous, but still convinced I was doing the right thing, "we may have to help her without her knowing we're doing it."

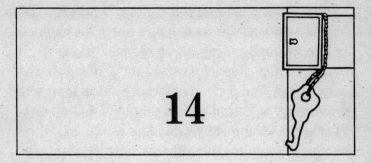

14

Dear **D**iary:

As it turned out, I got my chance to help Claudine sooner than I thought. I came home from school on Monday and found a note stuck in the side door. (The door Claudine uses coming in and out of the house.) I thought the note might be for me, and so I pulled it out.

The paper was folded in half, then in quarters. Written on the outside was "Claudine." Now at this point I knew the note wasn't for me. At this point I should have just stuck it right back where I found it and forgot about it.

But I didn't. What I did was the exact opposite. I opened the note and read what was written inside.

Claudine darling,
Tried to call, but no answer. Meet me at Avril at 7 for your birthday surprise.
Love, B.

Today was Claudine's birthday! And this "B" person, whoever he was, had a surprise planned for her. A really nice one, it seemed, since Avril was this fancy French restaurant a few suburbs away. Mom and Dad went there once for their anniversary and said it was fabulous.

I tried to imagine how Claudine would feel when she came home and found this note. Happy, for sure. Who wouldn't like somebody taking them out for a romantic dinner on their birthday? This bothered me. A romantic dinner might be just the thing to make Claudine think she liked this guy more than Laurent.

I still had so many unanswered questions about Claudine's life. Like, if she really loved Laurent, why was she here in America, and not back in Paris with him? I knew she liked her job with Roth Frozen Foods, but weren't there good jobs in France, too? Or why didn't Laurent just find a job here? Why did they have to live a million miles apart so Claudine could get lonely and be susceptible to the charms of guys named "B"?

I didn't know the answer to any of these questions. All I knew was that I was holding more than a piece of paper in my hand, I was holding an opportunity. An opportunity to get "B" out of the picture and help Claudine and Laurent stay together like I knew they should be.

If Claudine didn't get the note, she wouldn't

know about her birthday dinner. If she didn't know about it, she couldn't very well show up for it. "B" would wait at the restaurant then, when Claudine didn't show up, he'd have to think that she wasn't all that interested in him. Which I didn't think she was, not *really*.

This was scary, like holding someone else's fate in my hand. If I put the note back where I'd found it, Claudine's life would go along its own way. If I took it, I'd be changing the course of her events.

I put the note back.

Then I stared at it for a long, hard minute. I wished like crazy that Nancy were with me so I could ask her what she thought we ought to do. But Nancy wasn't there. I had to make this decision on my own, now, fast, before anyone came along and saw me standing there, debating what to do.

In the end, I felt my hand reach out and take the note and put it in my pocket.

I didn't let myself think about what I'd done. I couldn't. I had dinner with my family and then went upstairs to do my homework. Nancy called and wanted me to come over, but I said I couldn't. Really I was feeling too guilty and didn't want to tell her what I'd done. I was afraid even she would think I'd gone too far. I just wanted to be alone.

I sat at my desk, pretending that I was studying, but really just staring at the pages in my open math book. Josh and Adam were both out, which always brings the noise level in our house down considerably. It was really pretty quiet. Claudine's living room is right above my bedroom. Sometimes I can hear her walking around, sometimes I can hear her talking on the phone, but not the words. Right then though, I heard a different sound, one I'd never heard coming through from up there before. It was the muffled sound of crying. Not boo-hoo little crying. Big sobs crying.

I felt awful. I knew just what Claudine was crying about. And it was all my fault. When I'd taken the note, I'd only thought about getting rid of "B." I'd only thought of *him* sitting in the restaurant waiting for Claudine. I hadn't thought of where Claudine would be — up in her apartment thinking he didn't care about her birthday, didn't care about *her*.

I didn't know what to do. I reached into my pocket and felt the note. It was still there. I looked at the clock. It was already seven-fifteen. I was so torn. If I went up there and told Claudine what I'd done, she'd for sure be furious with me. It would probably end forever any chance I had of us being friends. On the other hand, I couldn't be so rotten as to let her go on crying up there when I knew I could make her stop just by handing her the note.

I went up the stairs and knocked softly on the door.

"Yes?"

"It's me. Elizabeth."

I heard her rustling around and blowing her nose and then she opened the door. For the first time, she wasn't looking stylish. She had on old jeans and a white T-shirt and her nose was red and her eyes redder. She was wiping them with a crumpled Kleenex.

"This is perhaps not the best time for a visit," she said.

"I know," I said. "And I'm the one responsible for it not being a good time."

"Whatever do you mean?" she said, clearly confused.

I took the note out of my pocket, handed it to her, and stood there while she read it.

"But how did you . . . ?"

"I found it stuck in the door when I got home from school. I stole it so you wouldn't know about B's surprise." I hung my head as I said this. There was no way I could look Claudine in the eye.

"But why would you want to make me so unhappy?" she said. "You don't seem like a mean girl to me. And I thought you were my friend!"

"I didn't. I'm not. I am," I stammered, but I knew I wasn't making any sense. To do that, I'd have to explain my motives to Claudine, which would involve letting her know how much snooping I'd been doing. Still, it was that, or having her think I was just one of the rottenest people in the whole world. And so I spilled the whole story — well, almost the whole story.

"It all started with your lamp," I said.

"My lamp?"

"Mom had me bring it up, and when I put it on your night table I couldn't help seeing the photo of Laurent. I just thought he was so cute."

"Oh, do you think so?" Claudine said. "I do, too, of course, but then I would."

"You do? You would?" I didn't get it. If she thought he was so cute, why was she throwing him over for this guy named "B"? But I went on with my story. I thought for a second and decided to skip over the part about bringing Nancy up and hiding in the pantry. It would just sound too weird. I went on to the next part, about finding the postcard.

"It was on top of all the other mail and so I really couldn't help reading it. And I could just tell from what he said how much Laurent loves you."

"Oh, I know he does," Claudine said, not seeming to be tortured by this knowledge one little bit. Maybe she really did have a hard heart under that nice exterior.

"Then I found a letter from him in the trash . . ."

"That's funny," she said, tapping her forehead with a finger, as if trying to remember something. "Usually I tear up my mail before throwing it away."

I rushed on so we wouldn't have to get into the part about me pasting the letter together again. "I could tell he was troubled and needed you to be there with him."

Claudine nodded. "Yes, this was true."

"What do you mean *was*?! It's still true. Laurent still loves you. He's still a wonderful person. That's why I did all this — to save you and Laurent!"

I don't know what I expected Claudine's response to all this to be. But I couldn't have predicted what actually happened.

She laughed. She started laughing and couldn't stop. I stood there with my mouth open.

"What's so funny?" I asked.

"You are saving me for Laurent?"

"Well, yes. He really loves you."

"Well, of course he loves me. He is my brother!"

"Your *brother*?! B-b-b-but I saw the photo and I thought . . . well, when you said there was a problem back home . . ."

"The problem is my father's business. He is

119

losing it. This has been weighing on my mind. Laurent has been trying to save it, but it's no use. I just received a letter today, though, which says Father has been offered a position with a larger company, so there may be a happy ending after all."

"Oh, no," I said in my smallest voice. "Have I ever goofed. If Laurent's not your boyfriend, I guess this guy here — this 'B' really is."

Suddenly Claudine grew very serious. "You must tell no one about this. Brian also works at Roth, and the company has a strict policy — no dating between employees. That is why I have been secretive about him. Oh, Elizabeth, I thought it was all over between us, that he would do nothing for my birthday. Now I see he has been wonderful, and is probably sitting there thinking I care nothing for him."

"What a mess I've made," I admitted, and started crying.

Claudine, being the wonderful person she is, put her arm around me. "I am not mad. I believe you really wanted to help. But you cannot help someone this way."

Then she took me by the shoulders and looked at me seriously. "You must promise me now that you will never do this kind of snooping again. You will see this as a lesson — what happens when you meddle in other people's lives. Even if I had been making a big mistake, it was mine to make."

"Claudine, you don't even have to make me promise. I am so sorry anyway. I'd never do anything like this again." And I meant it. My detective days were through. "Now, please," I begged her. "Get on the phone and call B — Brian — and tell him you're almost dressed and on your way to the restaurant. Tell him to put a plate on top of your soup to keep it warm. You can be there in half an hour if you hurry. Tell him some rotten, but not totally rotten, kid stole his note and at the last minute came to her senses."

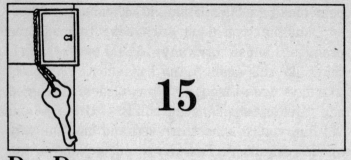

15

Dear **D**iary:

I waited on pins and needles to see what happened with Claudine and Brian after she went off to the restaurant. She must have gotten in after I fell asleep because I never heard her, and then the next morning when I left for school, her car was already gone.

That night, when I got back from the library, I found a note taped to my bedroom door. It was from Claudine and said to come up and see her.

She was all aglow when I got there. She made a little pot of tea and set it on her kitchen table with two cups and a plate of cookies.

"Please. Sit down, Elizabeth," she said, then began gushing about the night before — the dinner at Avril, how wonderful it was, how French, how romantic.

"And Brian saved a big surprise for the end. When the dessert came — a raspberry soufflé — the waiter brought another little plate with a small jeweler's box on it. Inside was this!"

She held out her left hand, and on the third finger was a small, very pretty diamond engagement ring. "Oh, Claudine! He asked you to marry him!"

She nodded happily.

"But what about those company rules?"

"That was Brian's other surprise. He's found a job with another food company in Detroit. We will no longer both be Roth employees."

"Oh, Claudine, I'm so happy for you," I said. "But wait. If you're getting married, that means you won't be living here."

She nodded. "We will have to find an apartment big enough for two."

"Boy," I said, shaking my head. "Everyone who lives up here winds up getting married. First Gram and now you. This is awful that you're leaving, just when we're getting to, you know, be friends."

"But I will still be here in Hampton Point. You can come visit me, the way you visit your grandmother. We will continue our friendship."

"Oh, Claudine, I'm so happy we still *are* friends. That is, I'm so happy I didn't ruin your life."

She reached over and gave my ear a good pinch. "No. You only *almost* ruined it. I hope they have taken away your detective's license."

"Don't worry," I told her. "I've retired from the

business for good. I'll never snoop on anyone again."

And I meant it, at least at that moment. But then, the next afternoon after school, when I saw Nancy and Samantha heading down to the basement soda and candy machines, I followed them and went around on the other side, to where the change maker was, so I could eavesdrop without being seen.

"I think it's very individualistic of you," Samantha was saying.

"You don't think it's just immature?" Nancy said.

"Oh, no! Besides, it's so much more healthful. And a good way to keep your weight down."

What could they be talking about?!

"Actually," Samantha went on. "I've been thinking that, come spring, I'm going to get my bike out of the basement and polish it up and start riding to school with you."

I just about burst out laughing. Samantha Howard riding her bike to school!? That'd be the day! She'd rather die than have someone see her riding a bike. She thinks they ought to give driver's licenses to twelve-year-olds. She always says she's been ready for a car since she was ten. Samantha is *way* beyond bikes.

How could Nancy believe this baloney? Couldn't

she see how fake Samantha was being, how fake this "friendship" was?

I knew I had to make her see what was going on. I must admit I'd been secretly happy when Ericka Powell told me that this whole friendship was just a scheme of Samantha's. But that was being happy for me, knowing I wasn't really losing my best friend. There was another side to it all, though. Ever since I talked to Ericka, I'd also been sad — for Nancy. I didn't like seeing her being made a fool of, which was essentially what Samantha was doing. I knew I had to put a stop to this.

I waited until after dinner, then went over to Nancy's house. She and her mom were in their living room, on the floor, working on one of their super-difficult jigsaw puzzles. Nancy may be slow at reading, but she can figure out a jigsaw puzzle about ten times faster than I can.

I hung out watching them for a while, then when Nancy's mother got a phone call and left the room, I grabbed my chance.

"Listen," I told Nancy, "there's something I've got to talk to you about. It's important." I told her what Ericka had overheard Samantha say.

"You're lying."

"I'm not."

"I just don't believe you," she said. I could see she was embarrassed and confused by what I was telling her.

"Look," I said. "I'm not telling you this to make you feel bad. It's not even *about* you, really. Samantha just wants to get back at us for seeing her in her big humiliating moment. She's always doing something rotten to someone, and you're just the latest someone."

"I still don't believe you."

"Let me prove it."

"How?" Nancy said, but still pouting.

"We put on a big fight scene in school. We do everything but knock each other down and pull each other's hair out. And we make sure to do this right in front of Samantha."

"I don't get it," Nancy admitted.

"If what Ericka said is true, if I'm right, Samantha will see she's busted up our friendship and her mission will be accomplished. And that will be the end of her need to have a 'friendship' with you. She'll drop you like a hot potato."

"I don't think you're right."

"Then what have you got to lose going along with my plan?"

Nancy thought about it for a minute, then said, "Okay, I'll do it. I just hope we can pull it off."

"Sure we can. Just think of all the times you've

really been mad at me. That ought to get you worked up enough to pull my hair a little."

We didn't get one chance the whole next day. Either Nancy and I were together and Samantha was nowhere to be seen, or we were in class, or I'd run into Samantha, but couldn't find Nancy. Finally, this morning, the perfect opportunity came along. Nancy and I were at our lockers hanging up our coats when Samantha came down the hall with Candace Quinn. I spotted them out of the corner of my eye and gave Nancy a swift kick in the ankle and nodded subtly over my shoulder.

"Now!" I whispered, and almost before I could finish the word, she grabbed me by the collar and spun me around and started shouting in my face, "Who cares what you think?! I'm sick of you being such a jealous friend!"

I grabbed onto her collar and shouted back, "And I'm sick of you being such an uncaring one, running off to hang out with her whenever she wants, leaving me behind!"

By this time Samantha and Candace, and a few other kids, had gotten within a few feet of us and had stopped in their tracks to witness our fight. We both pretended we didn't see them and just kept yelling at each other, throwing in every insult we could think of. If I didn't know it was a fake fight, I would have thought it was really real. We were doing a great acting job.

When I couldn't think of any more insulting things to say to Nancy, I put an exclamation point on the fight by slamming my locker door shut and glaring in stony silence at Nancy. Then we both saw it, out of the corner of our eyes and then, turning, we saw it full on. Samantha was nudging Candace in the ribs with her elbow and smirking. Clearly this fight was just what she'd been waiting for. Now Nancy could see what I'd said was true.

I turned and saw that she was crestfallen. "I really trusted that creep," she said in a sad, low voice to me. "But she turned out to be just rotten."

I put my hand on her shoulder and said, "But really, Nance, what else is new?" She turned to look at me and I could see the start of a smile, not on her lips, but at the back of her eyes. She was just beginning to see the humor in the situation. She was like the person who's slipped on a banana peel, was still hurting, but could imagine that from another point of view, she'd just looked silly, and that the whole thing was no big deal, really.

"Look at her, will you?" I said, nodding my head toward Samantha. "Samantha the Smug. She thinks she's ruined our friendship. What a zit."

I'd never called anyone a zit before. It just came to me in the moment, but somehow it perfectly captured Samantha standing there basking in her own happiness, thinking she'd ruined someone else's, when really she'd just fallen hook, line, and sinker for our big act.

Something about the stupid look on her face made both Nancy and I, at almost the same exact instant, begin to crack up. We started laughing so hard we fell against each other.

At first Samantha just stood there kind of shocked. Then, since she's no dummy, she figured out we were laughing *at her*, and if there's one thing Samantha can't stand, it's being laughed at. She glared at both of us, and then focused especially on Nancy and said, "Since you find me so amusing, Nancy, I really don't think it's going to be possible to continue our friendship."

"Oh, Samantha," Nancy said, catching her breath. "Go soak your head." And with that, she reached way into the back of her locker and pulled out the Marie Antoinette head with its red wig still attached, and tossed it across the hall at Samantha Howard, who, instinctively, from all her softball years of going for the ball, reached out and caught it.

It was — Dear Diary — a perfect moment.

After dinner, Nancy called and asked if I'd meet her at the Zephyr — her treat. We split a split, a banana split, that is. We've done this a thousand times. Neither of us said anything directly, but we both knew that tonight it was kind of a ceremony — to say we were best friends again.

So, Dear Diary, everything is okay . . . for now. Claudine and B are together, and so are Nancy and me.

Lizzie and Nancy are roommates — and it may be the end of their friendship! Read Dear Diary #5: The Roommate.

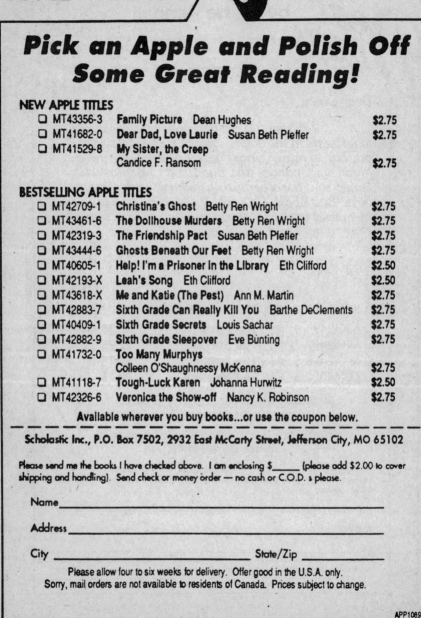

by Ann M. Martin

The seven girls at Stoneybrook Middle School get into all kinds
of adventures...with school, boys, and, of course, baby-sitting!

☐ NI43388-1	#1	Kristy's Great Idea	$2.95
☐ NI43513-2	#2	Claudia and the Phantom Phone Calls	$2.95
☐ NI43511-6	#3	The Truth About Stacey	$2.95
☐ NI42498-X	#30	Mary Anne and the Great Romance	$2.95
☐ NI42497-1	#31	Dawn's Wicked Stepsister	$2.95
☐ NI42496-3	#32	Kristy and the Secret of Susan	$2.95
☐ NI42495-5	#33	Claudia and the Great Search	$2.95
☐ NI42494-7	#34	Mary Anne and Too Many Boys	$2.95
☐ NI42508-0	#35	Stacey and the Mystery of Stoneybrook	$2.95
☐ NI43565-5	#36	Jessi's Baby-sitter	$2.95
☐ NI43566-3	#37	Dawn and the Older Boy	$2.95
☐ NI43567-1	#38	Kristy's Mystery Admirer	$2.95
☐ NI43568-X	#39	Poor Mallory!	$2.95
☐ NI44082-9	#40	Claudia and the Middle School Mystery	$2.95
☐ NI43570-1	#41	Mary Anne Versus Logan (Feb. '91)	$2.95
☐ NI44083-7	#42	Jessi and the Dance School Phantom (Mar. '91)	$2.95
☐ NI43571-X	#43	Stacey's Revenge (Apr. '91)	$2.95
☐ NI44240-6		Baby-sitters on Board! Super Special #1	$3.50
☐ NI44239-2		Baby-sitters' Summer Vacation Super Special #2	$3.50
☐ NI43973-1		Baby-sitters' Winter Vacation Super Special #3	$3.50
☐ NI42493-9		Baby-sitters' Island Adventure Super Special #4	$3.50
☐ NI43575-2		California Girls! Super Special #5	$3.50

For a complete listing of all the Baby-sitter Club titles write to:
Customer Service at the address below.

Available wherever you buy books...or use this order form.

Scholastic Inc., P.O. Box 7502, 2931 E. McCarty Street, Jefferson City, MO 65102

Please send me the books I have checked above. I am enclosing $ _____
(please add $2.00 to cover shipping and handling). Send check or money order — no cash or C.O.D.s please.

Name _____

Address _____

City _____ State/Zip _____

Please allow four to six weeks for delivery. Offer good in U.S.A. only. Sorry, mail orders are not available to
residents of Canada. Prices subject to change.

BSC790